OCCUPIED

KURT BLORSTAD

D0170094

Odin Publishing
Annapolis, Maryland

OCCUPIED
Copyright © 2019 Kurt Blorstad

Print ISBN 978-1732632400

Odin Publishing
Annapolis, Maryland

Cover by Book Cover Express
Licensed cover images: boys © Tomsickova / stock.adobe.com;
Planes © David / stock.adobe.com; Clouds
© Avantgarde / stock.adobe.com

For those who lost a family member during World War II, those who fought back against the German occupation of their country, and those who did not survive.

Other Works by Kurt Blorstad

Plane Excitement, July 2017

A collection of short, funny tales about interesting people the author has encountered while traveling. All profits from this book benefit the National Hemophilia Foundation.

"The one common undertaking and universal instrument of the great majority of the human race is the United Nations. A patient, constructive, long-term use of its potentialities can bring a real and secure peace to the world."

—Trygve Lie, First Secretary-General of the United Nations

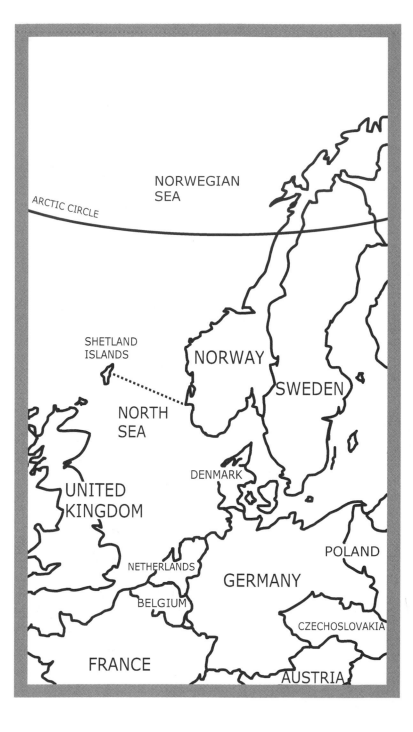

Acknowledgments

I would like to thank the following
people for helping with this book:
Trygve Blorstad
Thoralf Blorstad
Odd Blorstad
Thelma Blorstad Sampson
Carolyn Sampson Lenz
David Blorstad
Stanley Blorstad
Angela Blorstad Ruiz
Knut Ellenes
Oyvind Reiersen
Torstein Reiersen
Berit Reiersen
Wenche Storaker
Annmarie Throckmorton
Diana R.A. Morris
Erika Fine
Stephanie Barko
Gwen Gades
Karen Davis
Sue Dippel

And my beautiful wife, Carol Blorstad

PART 1

August 1, 1999

For my dad Trygve's 70th birthday, we traveled to Norway to visit relatives we had not seen in years. I told him that I wanted to visit all the places that I had heard about in his stories, mostly to see if he remembered things as they were, or if he—like most parents—had exaggerated what it was like when he grew up. I have realized that age and perspective greatly influence how people remember things, and everyone's parents tell embellished stories, like the one about walking to school in the snow uphill both ways for miles. My dad had plenty of those, and it was now time to see if things were as he had told me—not to prove him wrong, but to know what it was really like for him growing up in Norway during the German occupation.

We spent the first few days visiting relatives and seeing the great things Norway has to offer. As we made our way across southern Norway from Oslo to Bergen, we stopped in Spangereid to see his grandparents' house. This is where my dad and his brothers lived for a few years before they moved to another town just outside of Vanse. After arriving in Vanse, we first visited the graveyard where most of his maternal relatives were buried and then went to the one-room schoolhouse about half a mile away. Both places were exactly as he had described them, and as we stopped at each, he shared a little story about his experiences, smiling at the memories of his boyhood.

After visiting the graveyard and schoolhouse, we drove up a hill to the house he had lived in with his mom, grandmother, brothers, and sister. When we stopped the car in front of the house, it was as though he had never left. He started telling me stories, but now he was speaking only in Norwegian. Because I do not speak Norwegian, I understood very little, but his excitement needed no translation. Taking note of the tone of his voice and his lively gestures, I did not want to remind him that I needed additional clues to appreciate more fully what he was saying.

Soon he stopped speaking and pointed to the top of the hill, quickly getting out of the car and jogging up. When he reached the top, I reminded him that although English was his second language, it was my only language. He looked at me, smiled and laughed, and then said, "This is a very emotional spot for me. Many things happened at the top of this hill and on or behind these three rocks, many of which no one else alive knows about."

"Like what?" I asked.

"Here," he said, "sit with me and I will tell you what I have only ever shared with my mom—and that was only after she had passed away and I visited her and Pop at their graves."

May 2, 1936

It was an unusually warm day in May for southern Norway, and I was sitting on the edge of the dock with my older brother, Thoralf. He was eight years old, and I was seven. The air was damp, there was fog suspended over the fjord, and we could not see the other shoreline even though it was only half a mile away. Thoralf and I sat patiently on the wooden pier with our legs dangling over the edge; they were not yet long enough to reach the water just two feet below us. Bestefar, our grandfather on my father's side, had taken Mom and our three-year-old brother, Odd, in the rowboat to the bus station just across the fjord. We were awaiting his return to pick us up so we could join them. Thoralf and I were discussing what we would miss the most now that we were leaving Spangereid. It was the only home either of us could remember.

"I am not sure why we have to go," I said. "I mean, I am very happy here. I know that Pop had to go back to the United States, but why couldn't he have taken all of us with him?"

"Mom said it's because he needs to get things ready, like getting us all a place to live and making some money so we can pay for the boat trip," Thoralf replied.

"Do you think they will have lefse and fish cakes where we are moving to?" I asked.

"I am sure they will, but if not, Mom will show them how to make them. I just hope that they have fyrstekake there. I love helping Bestemor make it. The smell of the cinnamon and cardamom mixed in with all of that almond filling…"

Thoralf closed his eyes and paused to take a deep breath, as if a fyrstekake was right in front of him. "It's my favorite dessert in the whole world!"

"Mine, too!" I said, imagining the treat.

In the distance, I could hear the faint strokes of oars across the water, each a little louder than the last. Then I seemed to smell apples cooking, but it wasn't apples; it was Bestefar's pipe tobacco. I knew that smell from sitting on his lap as he told me stories about his adventures in the merchant marines. Bestefar was a great man of the sea, and after each of his journeys to faraway places, he would sit both of us on his lap and tell us about the fascinating places he had visited and the amazing things he had seen while at sea. He said that all good Vikings were men of the sea and that both of us would one day follow suit.

Moments later, I saw the small wooden rowboat that my brother and I had decorated with shields and a dragon's head break through the fog, now with only Bestefar in it.

Bestefar turned his head and called out to us, "Thoralf, Trygve, are you boys ready for your adventure?"

We looked at each other, confused.

"Aren't we just going to the bus station across the fjord?" I asked.

"Well, of course you are," Bestefar replied. "This boat trip is the first part of your journey to meet your other relatives, the ones from your mother's side of the family. It will be a great adventure with new places to see and people to meet! You will have great experiences and new stories to tell, just like I do every time I go to sea."

"Oh, yes!" We both replied. If Bestefar thought it was going to be fun, then it was going to be.

He tossed us the bowline and we pulled the boat tight to the dock with a thud. Thoralf and I handed him our luggage, which was tied closed with twine because the latches no longer worked. We climbed into the boat and sat where we'd sat so often before, when fishing with Bestefar.

As we pushed off from the pier, Bestefar said he was getting tired from all the rowing and asked if the two of us wanted to take over. We moved quickly, excited to change seats with him. The small rowboat rocked abruptly, as we both wanted to row from the starboard side. The seat on the port side just seemed a little less comfortable. In everything we did together, Thoralf and I seemed to compete over where we were going to sit. On this day I lost and had to row from the port side.

Bestefar reminded us that it was not a race and that if we did not work together, we would only be going in circles. Thoralf reminded him that we had rowed this boat many times before and knew how to work together. Pop had told us how important this was before he left. He also told us that we were the men of the family while he was gone and that we had to be responsible for and help take care of Mom and Odd.

Bestefar nodded, saying that our father was right and that he knew we would do a good job. Then he pointed us in the right direction, and with a small course correction, we were on our way.

The farther we rowed, the foggier it got. Everything in the boat, including our clothes, was wet from the dampness in the air. Bestefar reassured us that he knew exactly where we were and then adjusted his hat, stirred the tobacco in his pipe with a match, and relit it. He puffed on the pipe a few times to make sure it was lit and said, "The two of you are the best crew I have ever had. I am going to miss you both."

He turned his head and wiped his eye with a handkerchief. "Keep rowing," he said. "We will be ashore soon."

As we approached the shore, I heard what sounded like fish jumping out of the water. Then I heard Odd's voice call out, "Look, a boat!"

When I turned to look at him, I could see him and Mom waiting on the shoreline. He was throwing small rocks into the water, creating the noise that sounded like fish jumping. Thoralf and I stopped rowing and let the boat drift in. We heard the bottom of the boat scraping as it started to run aground on the small rocks near the shoreline. Thoralf and I jumped out to make the boat lighter and pulled it ashore. Bestefar climbed out and tied the boat to a big rock nearby before handing us our luggage.

With our belongings in hand, we all walked up the rocky shore to the road and then headed to the bus stop to wait for the bus to Vanse, the town nearest to where my mother grew up and the last stop for the bus. Mom and Odd were falling behind as Odd kept stopping to pick up rocks to throw into the water. Just after a bend in the road, I spotted a small red wooden building with a few benches around the outside. When we reached the bus station, we all sat down, except for Odd, who played with a stick he had found on the ground next to the bench.

Before long, I heard the engine of a bus as it came around the bend and pulled up in front of the station. The bus was not very big. It was green with red wooden spoke wheels, a luggage rack on the roof, and mud splashed down the side.

When it came to a full stop in front of the station, the doors opened, and an older gentleman stepped off and walked to the back. Then the driver got off and climbed up the rusty ladder that was attached to the rear of the bus. Once on the roof, he took down a bag and handed it to the man standing there. The man thanked the driver and walked into the bus station.

The driver called out, "This bus is going to Lyngdal, Farsund, and then on to Vanse. If that is where you are headed, please hand up your luggage so I can tie it down. We will be leaving in 10 minutes."

We walked to the back of the bus, and Bestefar handed up the luggage as we passed each piece to him. Mom had the tickets in her hand and told us to give Bestefar a hug and to thank him for letting us live with him and Bestemor and for all the fun times we had. Thoralf and I raced to give him a hug while saying we really did not want to go. He and Bestemor were the only grandparents we had ever known.

He hugged us back and then reached into the small burlap bag that he often carried with him and pulled out two books and some pencils. He gave Thoralf and me a book and three pencils each, explaining that Bestemor had bought each of us a journal. She wanted us to write about all the new people and places we saw and the things we did so that when we came back to visit, we could tell her about our adventures. We both promised we would do that and hugged him again. Next, Odd came over and handed Bestefar the stick he had been playing with, followed by a hug. Bestefar thanked him and reached into the bag once more and pulled out a small wooden boat that he had carved. Odd took it and started to walk back toward the water, but Mom grabbed him and said, "We can see it float when we get where we are going."

As we said our goodbyes, Mom handed us our tickets and told us to get on the bus and save her a seat. She then hugged Bestefar and said she was sorry that we all had to go. But, she explained, since Pop had gone back to the United States and hoped to make enough money for us to move back there with him, she wanted to spend some time with her family in Vanse. Her mom was alone now that her youngest daughter had married and moved out, and she could use some help with things.

Bestefar said that he knew why she was really going and that it was okay. Mom and Bestemor had been arguing more since Pop had left, and at one point Bestemor said that Mom was the reason Pop went back to the U.S.

At that moment, the bus driver announced, "Everyone please get on board. It is time for the bus to leave."

Mom hugged Bestefar, kissed him on the cheek, and boarded the bus.

As the bus driver closed the door, Mom walked to the back where we were sitting. The bus sputtered a few times and then backfired and lurched forward. It sounded worse than Mr. Selvig's tractor. Mr. Selvig lived next door to Bestefar and was always trying to fix his tractor. He spent more time working on it than riding it.

As the bus pulled away, we all waved goodbye to Bestefar through the window. He took off his hat and waved it and then lit his pipe as he walked back to the rowboat.

The ride started off slow as the bus's engine seemed to sputter and cough a lot. The four of us sat in the back row on uncomfortable wooden seats, Thoralf and me on one side and Mom and Odd on the other. Thoralf had gotten to the seat first and sat by the window, leaving me to sit on the aisle. Mom sat on the aisle of her side so she could contain Odd and keep him from falling off the seat. The bus had 11 other people on it. I had counted them. As the journey started, I wondered if they were all going where we were.

Mom looked at me and asked to see the journal I was given. I handed it to her. She said that it was a very nice present for Bestemor to give us and that we should take good care of them and start writing right away. She handed the journal back to me, and I opened it up. The black leather was very shiny, and the paper was crisp and white with lines on it. I took the pencil and carefully wrote my name on the first page. I wanted to start writing more but did not know where to start. I turned and asked Mom what I should write about.

She thought for a second and then replied, "Well, I think first you should write about yourself up until now. Like when and where you were born and then start with the first thing you can remember doing. Here, let me help you."

Mom reminded me that I was born on August 1, 1929, in Brooklyn, New York. She, Pop, Thoralf, and I lived in a small two-story brick row house with her sister, Agny, who had first moved to the Norwegian neighborhood with her in 1925. They had both gotten jobs in a bakery down the street from the apartment they shared. When they first arrived in New York, it was a very busy time with lots of new construction. The buildings going up downtown were bigger and taller than anything in Norway.

Mom then told me that she worked six days a week for ten or more hours a day and had been sending money back to her family because her younger sisters, Alene, Klara, and Palma, and her brother, Tarald, were still living with her mom. There was not a lot of work in Norway, and times were hard for her family. The money she and Agny sent back was a big help to them.

Many of the construction workers lived nearby and, with a subway stop right in front of the bakery, it got very busy every day around 6 p.m. There was one man, Olaf, who would stop in every Friday after work and buy an almond coffee ring. He was also from Norway but had grown up in Spangereid. Mom was from Amdal, just outside Vanse, a poorer part of the country, but that did not seem to bother him. When Olaf came in to buy his coffee ring cake, he would wander around the bakery until Mom was free to wait on him. When other clerks in the bakery asked if he needed help, he would pretend not to know what he wanted, but when asked by Mom, he all of a sudden knew, and it would always be an almond coffee ring. Mom told me she often had to hide one earlier in the day so they would not sell out before Olaf came in to buy his.

One day when Olaf came in to buy his almond coffee ring, he asked if he could walk her home after work. She said yes. They dated for a while, and then on February 14, 1927, Olaf asked her to marry him. She accepted, and on April 16, 1927, they got married. They moved into a small apartment in a four-story brick building at 705 59th Street in Brooklyn. The apartment was close to the subway, so my father could easily get to work downtown. Mom went on to say that my brother Thoralf was born on March 4, 1928.

Everything was going well until October 24, 1929. "Black Thursday," she called it. Many people lost their jobs, and others were out of work soon afterward. Pop had just left working on the Chrysler Building to work on the Empire State Building and managed to keep his job until the renowned skyscraper opened in May 1931. Pop then took on odd jobs for a while, but after a few months of hard times and very little work, on August 1, my second birthday, they decided that things were not going to get better anytime soon and that we should move back to Norway with my father's family. My parents took the last of our savings and purchased tickets for all of us on the Stavangerfjord steamship and moved to Spangereid with my grandparents.

At this point in the story, all I had in my journal was that I was born in Brooklyn, New York, on August 1, 1929, that Thursday was black, and that we all moved to Norway to live with Bestefar. Mom laughed and said that was the perfect way to start my journal. She recommended that I add all the fun things I remembered about living with Bestemor and Bestefar in Spangereid, and that there would be even more things to write about after we moved to her mom's house in Lista.

I thanked Mom for helping me and for telling me about where I was born. Just as I turned to my journal to begin writing about the first time Bestefar took me fishing, the bus bounced and jerked. Mom suggested that I wait until we stopped moving, since a wobbly bus was not the best place to work on my journal.

She said, "Why don't you look out the window like your brother and see all the new things there are to see."

I handed her my journal and pencil and asked her to put them in her bag for safekeeping. She wrapped a handkerchief around them to store them safely.

Thoralf was kneeling on his seat with his face plastered against the window as he pointed out all the things he saw. I went over to the window and stood between the seats. I had never been on a bus before. We were going so fast—at least 30 miles an hour! The bus wound its way up the hill, and when it reached the top, we could see so far. The air was clear and the sky was a bold royal blue with an occasional wispy white cloud mixed in. As we started down the hill, we could see the fog over the fjords and lakes. It was as if the clouds had fallen to the ground and were taking a nap over the waters below.

Now that we were going downhill, the bus was traveling even faster. It was exciting! As we zoomed around the turns, I had to hold onto the seat or else I'd fall over. The bus hit a bump and bounced. Thoralf and I laughed and then Mom, with a stern look, asked us to sit in our seats and try to be quiet because we were not the only people on the bus. After saying this, she turned her head and smiled. After a few more turns, the bus began to slow down and then stopped. We were now in Lyngdal, a small town at the northernmost end of the fjord. We stopped at the bus station and picked up two more passengers and were soon on our way again. The next stop on our journey would be Farsund. We passed by many farms with sheep and goats grazing in large open fields with the occasional rock jutting out of the ground.

I started to get hungry. I was sure Thoralf was hungry too, but with all there was to see out the window, he hadn't yet noticed that his stomach was grumbling louder than I had ever heard it. As I turned to tell Mom, she said, "I have brought some lefse for us to share. Are the two of you hungry?"

"Yes," I responded. Mom always seemed to know when I was hungry. She reached into her carryall and pulled out a small brown paper bag that contained three pieces of rolled-up lefse. She handed one to me and one to Thoralf and said that she and Odd would share the third one. I took a bite and was surprised. It had a buttery sweet taste and was more like dessert than lunch. I asked Mom what she had put in it, and she told me that she used butter and cinnamon sugar before rolling it up. This was much better than the rice pudding that typically would have been inside.

"A special trip deserves a special treat," she said.

I quickly finished my lefse, and before I knew it, the bus was stopping again, and we had arrived at the station in Farsund. Everyone except the four of us got off there. I could hear the bus driver on the roof and the clunking of luggage as he moved bags around and handed them down to the passengers. When he was finished, he hopped back on the bus, walked to where we were sitting, and said, "It is just the four of you going to Vanse. We should be there in about fifteen minutes. The roads are pretty bumpy, so it will be a slow drive. Do you have family there?"

I quickly spoke up and said, "Yes, we are all going to live with my grandmother."

The bus driver said, "Well, it is a very lovely town. You will like it there."

He walked back up the narrow aisle to the front of the bus, and we pulled out of the station to continue our journey.

At some point I must have fallen asleep because I felt Mom tap me on the shoulder. Thoralf was nowhere to be found. I rubbed my eyes and asked where we were. Mom said we had arrived in Vanse and pointed to the row ahead of me.

"Wake your brother, and then go outside and get the luggage from the driver. Thoralf is asleep in the seat in front of you."

I reached over the seat and shook Thoralf.

"We're here! We're here!" I cried. "Come on. We need to help the driver with the luggage."

I ran to the front of the bus, down the stairs, and out the door. Thoralf was right at my heels. When we reached the rear of the bus, the driver was on the ladder with one of our bags in his hand. He handed the first bag to Thoralf and said, "Take the bag over and put it on the sidewalk and then come back and help your brother with the rest."

I was not sure what he meant—I was just as big as my brother and could easily handle a bag by myself. I grabbed the next bag and took it to the sidewalk. I got there just as Mom and Odd did. Then Thoralf and the bus driver removed the last of the luggage from the bus and placed it next to us. The driver tipped his hat and said to Mom, "Have a good day," before walking into the bus station.

I asked Mom how far it was to Bestemor's house. She said just over two miles up the mountain. She explained that she had written to her mom and brother telling them what time we would arrive—her brother would pick us up. I saw a truck coming down the road and asked Mom if that could be her brother, Onkel Tarald.

"No," she said, "he does not have a truck."

Just then I heard a horse whinny and saw it come around the corner of the bus station.

"There is my brother," she said excitedly. "And there are his horses, Freya and Ord."

The two horses were pulling a cart with a small amount of hay in the back. It was not very big, and the wheels wobbled slightly as it pulled up in front of us.

Onkel Tarald jumped off and gave Mom a big hug. He then turned to us and said, "Well, you must be the three nephews your mom has told me so much about in her letters."

"Hi!" I said, "I'm Trygve! This is my brother Thoralf and my little brother Odd. Do you like to fish? Can you take us fishing like Bestefar used to?"

Onkel Tarald smiled and chuckled.

"Why yes, I do like to fish, but the farm keeps me very busy. If you help me with some of the farm chores, then I will have some free time to take all of you fishing."

Thoralf quickly spoke up. "I can help, too!"

"Well, of course you can. You can never have too much help on a farm, and I can use all the help I can get."

He grabbed the luggage and put it in the back of the wagon and told Thoralf and me to climb in the back, too. He then helped Mom and Odd into the front to sit with him.

We rode through the small town of Vanse. The streets were made of dirt, and there were several two-story white buildings on each side. I must have missed most of the town while asleep on the bus because we quickly reached the end. The wagon turned and headed out of the town. Just outside the town was a large church. Mom pointed to the graveyard and told us that, when she was younger, she would walk down to the church every week to water the flowers on her father's grave. She paused for a second and then asked in a sad voice if one of us would like to do that now that we were here. Mom did not talk much about her father, but when she did it was always about how hard he worked and how well he took care of the family, and it was always in a somber tone. I said I would do it for her if she would show me how.

After we passed the church, we came to a fork in the road and turned left to go up a hill. Mom told us that, had we turned right, the school we would attend was just around the corner and that it was all downhill from her mom's house to the school. Onkel Tarald said, "Hopefully, you and your brothers won't race to school like your mom did with our sister, Agny."

"What do you mean?" I asked.

"Well, it was many years ago, but your mom and our older sister were always competing with each other. One morning your mom was running late to leave for school and Agny left without her, saying that she was going to get to school first today. Your mom and aunt are both great skiers."

I interrupted Onkel Tarald. "What do you mean great skiers?"

"This is why your mom said it was all downhill to school from the house—once the snow came each winter, they skied to school." he continued his story. "Now, even with Agny's lead, your mom got her skies on quickly and headed down the hill to school. I was not there, but Agny was skiing down the road, which is the safest way to get to school, but not wanting to lose, your mom took a more direct path. Agny said that the next thing she knew, your mom came out of the trees by the Hansen farm and was now in front of her."

Mom quickly corrected him and said that Agny had fallen coming around the corner and she had stopped to help her up and that is really why she won.

"Besides," she said with a smile, "if Mom had found out that I had gone through the woods, she would have taken my skis from me for a month, and it was really cold that winter. I would have frozen if I had to walk."

Onkel Tarald laughed. "Yeah, that is what happened, and she is sticking to it."

This was a side of my mom I had never heard about, but I would soon learn it was also a part of me.

As we continued along our path, the road was very narrow in some spots with a few wild flowers starting to bloom along the side. They looked as if they were growing right out of the rocks.

As we crested the hill, Mom pointed and said, "There it is. There is Bestemor's house. You are going to love living here."

It did not look as big as the house we had just left in Spangereid. As we got closer, I could see it was a one-story building with white wooden siding and a reddish-brown tile roof. There was a stone foundation visible from one corner, but the rest of it was hidden because the house was cut into part of the hill. Two people were standing at the top of the stone staircase in front of a big red door with an elm tree on the left side of the stairs and a large lilac bush on the right side. As we got even closer, I could see that behind the lilac bush was a set of stairs going down to a cellar. This would be the house I would remember the most as a young boy in Norway.

As we pulled up to the house, Bestemor, my mom's mother, came down the stairs to greet us with Tante Anna, Onkel Tarald's wife. Bestemor still had her apron on and smiled warmly as she walked over to hug us. She told us to come inside because dinner was almost ready.

I followed Mom up the stone stairs and through the big red door. As I stepped inside, I could smell what I thought was fish frying, along with a slight sooty smell. The foyer did not seem very big because there were seven of us standing in it. From where I was, I could see a door that was closed to my left, a parlor to the right, and the kitchen straight ahead with the table already set for dinner, with a basket of bread and lit candles down the center. Bestemor then asked us to go in the kitchen and sit down. Thoralf and I raced to the table to find two benches—one on each side—a chair at one end of the table, and the other end pushed up tight against the wall. Thoralf and I knew better than to sit in the chair at the head of the table, as it must have been for Bestemor.

We both raced to the far side of the table to sit on the end of the bench closest to the chair. I once again lost out and decided to sit in the same spot on the other bench. I wanted to be next to Bestemor. As I sat, Tante Anna came in and asked if I would like to move over and sit between her and Onkel Tarald. She said that whoever sat on the end of the table had to get up and help get the food and, since it was my first day here, I might not know where everything was. I slid over to sit between her and Onkel Tarald, and Mom and Odd sat on the other side of the table next to Thoralf.

The wooden plank table was a little rough, while the benches were smooth from years of use. I noticed another chair in the corner of the kitchen with a hat hanging on the back of it. I asked Bestemor whose hat it was and why the chair was not at the table. She looked at Mom and then turned to look at me. "That was Bestefar's hat and the chair he sat in when we had dinner. He died from the Spanish flu when your mom was very young. I leave it there to remember him. He was happiest when he sat down for a good meal after a long day's work."

Bestemor then said to Mom, "Please say grace."

"In Jesus's name we sit at the table," Mom began, "to eat and drink according to Thy word. To your glory, Lord, for gifts given. We receive food in Jesus's name. Amen."

After we said grace, Mom passed around the basket of bread, and Tante Anna took the food out of the oven. She served each of us a piece of fish while Bestemor followed behind and scooped out rutabaga and potatoes. The fish tasted better here than in Spangereid. Mom said it was because Bestemor was the best cook in the whole town and she was also the best spinner—everyone nearby would bring her their wool to spin into yarn. This explained the big wheel I saw in the parlor.

Thoralf and I finished our dinner and asked if we could be excused. Onkel Tarald looked at Mom and said that he could use some help getting the trunks off the wagon. Mom gave Onkel Tarald the look that Thoralf and I had seen often when Mom was not happy, the one with her head slightly down and turned a little to the right with her eyes looking right through you. I was glad that this time the look was for Onkel Tarald and not me. She said it would be okay this time, but to remember that we were supposed to stay at the dinner table until everyone had finished eating. Thoralf and I thanked Bestemor and Tante Anna for making dinner and jumped up to help Onkel Tarald. As we walked to the door, Bestemor told us to take the trunks upstairs because we would all be staying in the room in the attic. I didn't know there was an upstairs, but as I approached the front door, I noticed the narrow stairway. I hadn't seen it before because when the front door is open, it blocks the entrance to the stairs.

As we walked down the stairs outside, Onkel Tarald said, "We have forgotten about Freya and Ord. They need to have dinner, too. Trygve, go to the well and get them some water. Thoralf, come here and help me get the hay."

The well was between the house and the dirt road where the horses were. There was a hinged wooden cover atop the three-foot-tall stone surround. A bucket was placed upside down on top of it with one end of a long rope tied to its handle and the other end tied to a wooden post through a pulley on a beam above the well. I opened the cover and dropped the bucket down into the well. After a few seconds, I heard the bucket splash into the water. I waited for it to fill and started pulling it back up. It was now very heavy. I pulled with all my strength and was making good progress when Onkel Tarald came over to help me. Together we pulled the bucket out of the well and poured it into another bucket he had brought over from the wagon. He told me to close the cover on the well, coil the rope up, and place the bucket upside down on top of the rope just as I had found it. "When winter comes," he said, "you will know why it should be done that way."

By the time I had done all of that, he and Thoralf had fed the horses, put most of the luggage inside, and were walking up the stone stairs with the last trunk in hand. I quickly ran and caught up with them. Once inside with the front door closed, we started to carry the luggage up the dark narrow stairway. I asked where the light switch was, and Onkel Tarald chuckled.

"This house does not have electricity," he explained. "Only the buildings in and near the town have electricity."

He called for Tante Anna to bring an oil lamp. She came with the lamp and went up first as we followed behind with the luggage. When we reached the top of the stairs, she opened the door on the right side of the hallway. It was now not as dark as it had been in the windowless hallway because there was a window at the far end of the room allowing light to spill in. The room had sloped ceilings on both sides with a small area of flat ceiling just high enough for Onkel Tarald to stand up straight. There was a metal stovepipe in one corner that went into the brick chimney just below the ceiling. I saw only three beds, two small dressers, and a chair with another oil lamp and some matches on it.

As I looked around I heard Onkel Tarald say it was time for him and Tante Anna to go. We went back downstairs, and everybody said goodbye. Mom said it had been a long day and she was tired. It was now time for all of us to go to bed.

As we walked upstairs, I asked Mom if I could have the bed on the right, and then Thoralf said that he wanted the bed on the right. Mom replied that we could both have the bed on the right because we were to share a bed. She and Odd would share a bed, and Bestemor would be sleeping in the third bed, closest to the door. She had not liked the past few months living alone and was happy to have roommates again.

After saying our prayers, Thoralf and I jumped into bed. This time there was no fighting over which side each of us got. We slept on our sides, back to back, with Thoralf facing the wall and me the center of the room, just as we had slept at Bestefar's house in Spangereid. Once we were settled, Mom blew out the lamp, and I soon fell asleep.

May 3, 1936

When I woke up, I saw that Bestemor was not in her bed, but Mom and Odd were still asleep in theirs. I got out of bed to get dressed and stood on the bare hardwood floor. The plank next to the bed was loose and squeaked as I stood on it. Roused awake by my movement and the squeak of the floor, Thoralf rolled over and asked where I was going.

"To find Bestemor and see if she needs any help," I replied.

Thoralf rolled to the edge of the bed, sat up, and stretched.

"Wait a second and I will come with you," he said with a yawn.

Once dressed, the two of us headed downstairs and could hear Bestemor in the kitchen as we rounded the corner. We walked in, said good morning, and asked if she needed any help.

"Yes," she said. "I need two cakes from the root cellar to make breakfast."

We walked over to the stairs but only saw stairs going up to where we slept and none going down. I walked back into the kitchen and asked Bestemor how to get to the root cellar. She told us that there was a door outside just under the front stairs and that there was also a trap door under the bench of the kitchen table for when the weather was bad. Thoralf and I raced over to the table, slid it over, moved the bench out of the way, and there it was! I grabbed the metal loop and pulled the door up, leaning it against the wall. I looked down into the dark cellar and turned to Thoralf to tell him he could go first. He looked down the hole for a moment and then climbed down the wooden ladder. When he got to the bottom, I started to follow.

Bestemor called after us, "The cakes are right at the bottom of the ladder on your left as you climb down."

When I got to the bottom of the ladder, I turned to see Thoralf standing by a large black kettle. It sat on top of a patch of stone floor near the back of the cellar. I looked around and saw that the floor was a mixture of stones and dirt and the walls were all stone. There were two narrow windows at the front wall, flush against the underside of the exposed wooden floor joists of the first floor. I could see a door that must have been the one Bestemor told us led outside. It had a narrow sidelight to one side. With these three small windows, there seemed to be just enough light to see everything in the cellar, but I could not see any cakes.

Just then Bestemor called down to us and said to hurry up before the fire in the stove went out. I was not sure what that meant, but I walked over to the ladder and asked her what the cakes looked like. She said that they were brown and shaped like a loaf of bread. I looked to the left of the ladder, as she had told us earlier, and saw exactly what she described. There must have been a hundred of them stacked in the corner.

Thoralf walked over to where I stood and said, "That is a weird way to store cakes."

I agreed. When I first heard there was going to be cake for breakfast, I was happy, but now I was not so sure about it. They did not look very tasty.

We each picked one up, headed back up the ladder, and handed them to Bestemor. She opened the firebox on the stove and threw them both in. Thoralf and I looked at each other, confused.

"Bestemor, why did you throw them into the fire box?" I asked.

"They are peat cakes, and peat cakes are better to cook with than wood because they burn with a steady heat," she replied. "You will learn more about them when you visit your onkel's peat bog and help us cut them from the ground."

She then said, "Why don't the two of you sit down at the table and I will get you some breakfast. I am making you eggs and potato pancakes."

I loved eggs, so I quickly sat down in anticipation. After we were seated, Bestemor walked over with two plates, each with one fried egg, a small potato pancake that had been fried in what smelled like lard, and a piece of bread. It looked and smelled delicious! We both said thank you, and Thoralf quickly dug into his plate while I savored the moment.

After I had finished my breakfast, I asked, "Where is Mom?"

Bestemor replied, "She is not feeling well this morning, so she asked me to make you breakfast."

I nodded. She must have been tired from our long trip yesterday.

After breakfast, Bestemor took Thoralf and me around the house and taught us what we needed to do each day to help out.

First we went out the front door and down the stone stairs. When we got to the bottom, we looked underneath and could see a small red door with a narrow sidelight at the bottom of another set of stairs. Thoralf and I had seen this door from the inside when looking for the peat cakes and now knew where it led. Bestemor said that this entrance was used mostly during the summer for stocking up for the winter. She turned and pointed to the well. I told her that Onkel Tarald had let me get the water for the horses yesterday and showed me how to place the rope and bucket when I was finished. Bestemor said that it looked as though I had done a good job. Then she turned and headed back up the stairs and through the front door.

We followed her through the entry and back into the kitchen. She pointed at the two buckets on the kitchen counter by the window and explained that they needed to be filled every day in the morning and again in the afternoon.

"I filled them already this morning," Bestemor said, turning and heading through a door next to the stove. This was a room we had not been in yet.

"This is the pantry where I keep most of the items I use each day," she explained, continuing the tour. When we first walked in, the room was dark because there was no window, but Bestemor opened a door that led outside, and light spilled in. I could see firewood stacked up against the wall opposite the door we had come through. On the other walls were lots of bins and a few wooden shelves. Some of the bins contained potatoes, carrots, rutabagas, and other assorted vegetables, while others were empty.

Now with light in the room, Bestemor pointed to an empty spot on the floor and said, "That empty space is where I want you to stack the peat cakes from the basement. After I finish showing the two of you around, I will need you to bring up 30 of them and stack them here. You should have to do this only every few weeks." she wiped her hands on her apron. "I am glad the two of you are here to help me. Maybe now I can catch up on all the chores."

As we walked out the back door and stepped down onto a stone landing, Bestemor pointed to her right and said, "There is the outhouse. The more you use it, the fewer chamber pots you will have to empty."

Thoralf and I looked at each other, not knowing what to say. Where we had just moved from we had never had to do that. Pop's mom took care of those sorts of things.

Bestemor turned left and proceeded to walk along a narrow stone path to the far corner of the house. There was a fenced-off area with weathered pickets that still had some remnants of white paint on them. She walked through the gate and opened a door that led back into the house. As we followed, I could hear chickens clucking and saw, to my surprise, that the hen house was actually part of the main house, just with an outside door.

As I walked in, I saw a mixture of wood chips and hay on the floor. I counted 15 cages made of wood and wire. They were five across and three high on the back wall, but I counted only 10 chickens. There were some bins filled with grain, a shovel, a hatchet, and other tools on the front wall beside the door with a narrow pathway between the two. Bestemor explained how often we needed to feed the chickens, how to collect the eggs so as to not get pecked, how often to clean the cages, and where to put the waste when we were finished.

"Here is the basket you are to put the eggs in," Bestemor said. "Make sure to use this basket when you bring them to me. We do not want to mix the baskets or the water pails that we use for the chickens with the ones we use for ourselves."

She told us that she usually traded most of the eggs for other things she needed, but today she wanted to have a special breakfast for us, so she kept most of them. As I listened, I thought to myself that we needed more chickens so we could keep more eggs for breakfast.

We walked out of the hen house and around to the left side of the house. Bestemor pointed at a rough patch of ground as she led us up the hill and said that now that we were all here to help, she could get the garden planted.

"It's the perfect time to plant potatoes, carrots, onions, and rutabagas. If there is anything you want planted, let me know, and I will ask around for the seeds."

As we neared the crest of the hill, I could see three medium-sized rocks of varying heights all in a row. Next to them were two hazelnut trees that looked more like bushes because they were not very tall. When we reached the top of the hill, the view was amazing! You could see all the way down to the shore. Bestemor said that when they were younger, Mom and Tante Agny would come up here and sit, looking off into the distance and wondering what it would be like to live in America. Many of their friends had left Norway hoping for a better life there.

Bestemor turned and headed back down the hill.

"Come on," she said. "The two of you know how that story ended. We need to get back to the house so you can start your chores."

Thoralf and I jumped off the rock we were sitting on and ran to catch up with Bestemor. As I walked in the back door of the pantry, I could see Mom and Odd sitting at the kitchen table eating breakfast. I asked her how she was feeling and if yesterday's long trip was why she had slept so late this morning. She replied that the trip was one reason she was tired but that we should sit with her at the table so she could tell us the other reason she was not feeling well.

The three of us sat at the kitchen table with Mom and Odd. Mom turned and looked at Bestemor. Bestemor smiled and nodded her head. "Go ahead. Tell them."

Mom turned back and looked at Thoralf and me. "I am going to have a baby."

Bestemor now had a big smile on her face as she grabbed Mom's hand with both of hers.

Thoralf shouted out, "Can this one be a girl? I have enough brothers, and it would be nice to have a sister to help with all the cleaning I have to do."

Mom laughed. "I will see what I can do about that. Besides, with your father being in America, there is no one here to teach another boy."

What Mom said made sense to Thoralf and me. She was also hoping for a girl so that she and Bestemor would have someone to hand down traditions to. Thoralf and I still had to help teach Odd what to do. Another brother to teach would mean less time for fishing and other things we enjoyed. Yep, we all agreed a sister is what we wanted.

"This is great news," Bestemor began, "but it is now time for the two of you to start your chores. Go out and get me more water from the well so I can clean up from breakfast, and then get the peat cakes out of the cellar and put them in the pantry where I showed you."

Thoralf went over to the counter and grabbed the two wooden buckets. He turned and handed one to me, and out the door we went.

June 25, 1936

Mom was feeling better in the mornings and was not as tired. By now, Thoralf and I had been doing our chores every day and gotten very quick at them. Bestemor seemed to know when we were finished, though, and always called to give us more tasks.

On this day, the weather was cloudy, but dry—it had not rained for several days. Thoralf and I were sitting on the front steps, and since the sun was up early this time of year, the steps were warm. Not wanting to go back inside, we looked off into the distance and talked about what we thought it would be like when we moved back to America.

As we talked, I heard a horse in the distance and turned to see Freya and Ord coming up the hill pulling the hay wagon with only Onkel Tarald in it. I immediately got up and ran to the well to get water for the horses so that they would have something to drink as soon as they got here.

When the wagon reached the house and came to a stop, Onkel Tarald stood up and said, "Well, lucky me, the two people I have come to get are here waiting for me and look ready to go."

"Go where?" Thoralf and I asked at the same time.

"Well, to help me on my farm. Today is a perfect day to cut peat for the winter," replied Onkel Tarald.

Just then, Mom opened the front door and stepped outside. "I was wondering when you were going to come by," she said.

Onkel Tarald jumped down from the wagon and walked up the stairs, rubbing Thoralf and me on the head as he passed us. He then gave Mom a big hug and asked how she was doing. Mom said that she was feeling better in the mornings now and was able to keep food down. He was glad to hear that and said that he needed some help today to cut and stack peat. Mom told him it would be okay for us to help but to make sure not to bring us home too late.

Hearing this, Onkel Tarald glanced at us. "Quick, boys," he said with a smile, "get up in the wagon before she changes her mind."

We both quickly jumped up into the front of the wagon and settled on the bench seat. Onkel Tarald joined us, grabbed the reins, and we were off.

As the wagon turned around to head back down the hill, Thoralf and I waved to Mom and said thank you. The wooden seat was smooth from wear and had a short back to lean against. It was not as comfortable as sitting in the back on the hay, but the view was much better. The ride down the hill on the short section of road was quick. When we came to the fork in the road, we went left to go up the mountain. I had only ever turned right to go down into town.

Soon after turning, we passed a small weathered white building with a covered front porch. There was a tall thin man wearing a white apron sweeping the front porch. As we passed him, Onkel Tarald waved and said, "Hello, Christian. Baking anything good today?"

I could now smell bread baking, and the aroma was making me hungry. It smelled as good as Mom's.

"Everything I bake is good," he replied. "Today I am making two types of bread and some rolls, and later I will be making cookies."

I was now very interested in meeting him.

"Hey, Onkel Tarald," I asked. "Who is this man?"

"Why that is Mr. Ellenes. He owns that little store and bakery. His store has assorted items that we farmers need, along with dry goods and what he bakes two or three days a week. He is in a good location. Most of us who live up the mountain do not want to go all the way into town to get the few things we need."

I quickly turned around as we passed him and shouted, "Hi, Mr. Ellenes! I am Trygve, and this is my brother, Thoralf. We are going with our Onkel Tarald to cut peat."

"Well, don't let him work you too hard, and make sure to stop by on your way back," he replied with a wave.

Just past the store was a small house and barn. Onkel Tarald told us it was Mr. Ellenes's farm and that he also raised sheep. He pointed off in the distance, and I could see the sheep in the field below.

Onkel Tarald started to tell us what we would be doing as we continued to his farm.

"Boys, today we will be cutting peat and stacking it to dry out. Then every two weeks or so we will turn and restack it so it dries evenly. When it's dry sometime in September, we will load up the wagon and take enough to my mom's house for the winter, and the rest I will store in the barn and cellar for my house," he explained.

I had wondered where the peat cakes came from and soon learned that it was not an easy job.

The road narrowed with spruce trees closing in on both sides. This wooded area was very dense, and you could not see far into the trees. It seemed endless. I could hear something in the woods but could not see what it was. Onkel Tarald said it was either deer or elk and not to be worried.

We were now at another fork in the road and this time turned right. I asked how much longer it would be, and Onkel Tarald said it was not much farther. We headed downhill, turned right again, and approached a large pasture with many sheep. Down the hill I could see a house. Onkel Tarald pointed to it. "There it is. That is where your Tante Anna and I live."

As we pulled up to the farm, we stopped briefly at the house. It was much larger than Bestemor's house and had a lot more windows. Decorative trim adorned all the openings, and beautiful lace curtains blocked my view inside. The house sat on a stone foundation like Bestemor's, but it was just two steps above the ground. There was a large barn, all weathered and grey, attached to the back of the house. I could hear chickens and see a few cows grazing next to it.

Tante Anna came outside to hand Onkel Tarald a basket with food for all of us. He jumped off the wagon, took the basket, and placed it and two water buckets in the rear of the cart. He also threw a few odd-looking shovels in the back of the cart, and then he jumped back in and we took off again. It was a short ride down a slight hill to a large flat area. We pulled up to what looked like a cliff and turned parallel to it and stopped. Now that we were close, I could see it was only about a four-foot drop.

We all jumped off the wagon and walked to the rear of it. The air down here was still and had a slight smell. It is hard to describe, but it's a little like the smell of wet leather shoes. Onkel Tarald handed me a straight, wide shovel, and he took a weird-looking L-shaped one. He walked to the edge of the drop-off and scratched several lines in the ground three feet apart while telling me to take my shovel and push it straight into the ground until the blade was all the way in. I was to do this all the way across the line he had just scratched. As I cut across the line, Onkel Tarald jumped down the four-foot bank. He took the L-shaped shovel and about six inches down pushed it horizontally into the bank and toward the cut I had made. He lifted the shovel out and came away with a perfectly shaped rectangle of peat that was six inches wide, six inches deep, and three feet long. He threw it up onto the bank by Thoralf.

He said to Thoralf, "I will do my best to place them so they are easy for you to pick up. If they break, don't worry. Just place the pieces back together when you stack them. Place five of them with a slight space next to each other, and then place five more on top of those turned across them. Stack them six rows high before you start another stack."

Thoralf looked a little overwhelmed, but as Onkel Tarald started cutting and throwing the peat logs up faster, my brother quickly figured it out. His first few stacks were a little crooked, but by the fourth he was able to stack a perfect cube. I, on the other hand, was using all of my strength to cut into the ground. Onkel Tarald would stop every once in a while because he had caught up to where I was. This went on for a while with very little conversation other than Onkel Tarald giving us directions.

When Thoralf finished his tenth stack, Onkel Tarald said, "Let's eat some lunch."

By this time, I was starving, and I am sure Thoralf was, too. As we put down our tools, I noticed that Onkel Tarald had cut the peat into a perfect set of stairs. He walked up it, and we followed him to the back of the wagon. He handed us each a cup, and we got water from the bucket while he cut a loaf of bread into several slices and opened a jar of strawberry jam. As Thoralf and I ate lunch, Onkel Tarald ate his while tending to the horses. When he finished, he came to the back of the cart and asked if we had enough to eat. Thoralf asked if he could have another slice, and

I quickly said, "Me, too." Onkel Tarald cut two more pieces off, handing one to each of us.

Suddenly he looked around as if he had lost something and took a step. Then he turned back around and said, "How about I tell you boys a story?"

As we ate, he told us about his father and how the two of them would cut peat, tend to the animals, and after a hard day's work go inside to a great dinner. He talked and talked, and when he was done, it was right back to work cutting peat, stopping only occasionally for a drink of water. We cut another 20 stacks before Onkel Tarald told us we could stop for the day. I was tired and walked slowly to the cart, dragging the shovel along the ground. The ride home seemed quick, but I am sure it was because I slept most of the way. When we got home, I climbed on Onkel Tarald's back, and he carried me inside. When we walked in the front door, Mom was waiting for us.

"What took you so long?" she asked.

"I lost track of the time, and the boys were doing such a good job I did not want to break the rhythm they had gotten into," Onkel Tarald said, his voice excited.

I went up to bed. Onkel Tarald and Thoralf walked into the kitchen with Mom as she scolded Onkel Tarald for keeping us so long.

August 28, 1936

On this day, after our chores, Mom told us it was time to sign up for school. She grabbed her bag and walked Thoralf and me down the hill to the little one-room schoolhouse. The school was on a piece of flat ground about a mile past the fork in the road that led up the hill to Mr. Ellenes's store. As we got closer, I could see a large white building with lots of windows. Thoralf said it looked like a church without a steeple, and he was right—that is exactly what it resembled. There was a big open field next to it with horses. As we walked up to the door, Mr. Dungvold greeted us.

"Well hello there, boys," he said warmly. "And who might you be?"

Thoralf and I introduced ourselves at the same time, our voices blending together. Then Mom spoke.

"Hello, Mr. Dungvold. I am Pauline, Paluda Andreassen's daughter. I am here to let you know that my two boys will be attending school here this year. Trygve is seven, and Thoralf is eight."

"Well, that is great. I love having new students and have plenty of room here for them," he replied. "Let's go inside to fill out some forms, and I will show them where they will be sitting."

As we walked in, it seemed as bright inside as it did outside. The tall windows soared to the ceiling, and on the two long walls, there seemed to be more window than wall. The front wall held a large chalkboard, and the back wall had a set of stairs that led to the attic.

The desks were arranged in four rows, with six desks in each. There was a larger desk just off center of the front wall. I could also see two small stoves, one at the rear of the building and the other near the desk at the front.

As I looked around, Mom finished filling out the forms for Mr. Dungvold, and he walked over to tell us that school started promptly at 10 a.m. We were not to be late.

"Trygve, you will be in second grade, and Thoralf, you will be in third," he explained. "We sit by rows, with the first graders starting on the left and then second, third, and fourth graders on the right. Grades one through four will go to school Tuesday, Thursday, and Saturday, and grades five through eight go to school Monday, Wednesday, and Friday."

I asked what time school was over, and he replied that it ended when everyone had finished their work. "If everyone is productive and does not dilldally, then it's usually around 3 p.m. I will ring the bell when school is over so your parents know to expect you. No goofing off on the way home. I am sure the two of you have lots of chores to do."

With a statement like that, Mr. Dungvold obviously knew Bestemor. We thanked him and headed home.

September 30, 1936

One Wednesday afternoon, Thoralf and I did not have school, so we walked to Onkel Tarald's to help load up the peat we had been turning to dry all summer. We stopped in to see Mr. Ellenes just in case he had anything like a loaf of day-old bread or maybe a broken cookie or two he wanted to share with us.

As we walked in, Mr. Ellenes was sweeping the floor. The fighting aromas of dust and freshly baked bread were in the air. I did my best to smell only the bread, but the occasional whiff of dust made that difficult.

"Hello, Trygve. Hello, Thoralf. What are the two of you up to today?" he said as he swept.

"We are headed to Onkel Tarald's to load up the peat cakes and take them to Bestemor's house," I replied.

Thoralf had walked away and stood in front of the tool section as Mr. Ellenes and I talked. He eyed all the shiny items and stared hard at a small coping saw that was used to cut curves in small intricate woodwork.

"What are you interested in, Thoralf?" Asked Mr. Ellenes.

"When we lived in Spangereid, Bestefar used to make birdhouses with a saw like this one," he answered, pointing to the coping saw.

"Yes, that is a fine saw for delicate work. I do not usually stock items like that, but the man who sells me tools gave it to me. I have no use for it, so it is there with the rest of the tools for sale. He gave me several blades for it, too. Let your Onkel Tarald know I have it—he may be interested." he paused. "Shouldn't you boys be on your way?"

"Yes, Mr. Ellenes, we need to go. Maybe we will stop here again when we pass by with the loaded wagon."

I grabbed Thoralf, and we went out the door and continued on our way.

When we arrived at Onkel Tarald's house, the wagon was full of hay and Onkel Tarald was on it, leading Freya and Ord around to the barn.

"Perfect timing, boys. You have arrived just in time to help me unload the hay into the barn, and then we can load it up with the peat cakes. If you do a good job, I think Tante Anna may have something for you."

I was not sure what it was going to be, but everything Tante Anna made tasted good. Thoralf and I ran around to the back of the barn. Onkel Tarald had pulled the cart inside right next to the loft. Thoralf, excited about a possible treat, grabbed a pitchfork and eagerly climbed to the top of the hay and started forking it into the loft.

Onkel Tarald called out, "Not so fast. I need to chock the wheels and feed the horses so they do not get anxious."

Just then, Freya whinnied, and the horses stepped forward and back. Onkel Tarald grabbed them by the reins, but it was too late. Thoralf lost his balance and rolled down the haystack and off the back of the cart. When I ran around to the back of the cart to see how he was, I found my brother lying flat on his back in a pile of hay with a half-smile on his face.

"I guess it's a good thing that most of the hay I was pitching missed the loft and ended up back here," he said.

Onkel Tarald, now standing beside me, just shook his head and laughed. "Well, if I ever need someone to unload the hay to the ground, I know who to ask. I think all of the hay you pitched landed there and not in the loft. Lucky for you, I see." he shook his head again. "Next time make sure the cart is secure before standing on top of it to work."

He reached down to help Thoralf up and told him to go up in the loft. "I'll pitch the hay up to you so you can pitch it to the back of the loft."

As Onkel Tarald climbed on top of the hay, he said to me, "Trygve, when I have made some space, you pitch the hay that is on the ground back into the wagon."

With Onkel Tarald now in the wagon and all of the hay going up into the loft, it was only a few minutes before we were done and on our way down the hill to load up the peat cakes. This time when the wagon stopped, Thoralf jumped off and chocked the wheels as I grabbed the feedbags.

Onkel Tarald laughed again and said, "I see you learned something today. Don't tell your mother how you learned it, or once again I will be on her bad side."

Thoralf and I looked at each other and then back at Onkel Tarald, and smiled. "We won't say anything to her," I said. "We like coming here and helping you."

Once we were done with the hay, we climbed on the cart and headed out of the barn. When we reached the front door, Tante Anna came outside and handed Onkel Tarald a basket. There was a sweet buttery smell coming from it. Onkel Tarald placed it on the bench between us, thanked Tante Anna, and motioned the horses to start down the hill. Thoralf and I were dying to know what was in the basket, and I could not wait any longer.

"Onkel Tarald, what is in the basket that smells so good?" I asked.

"Well, let's find out," he replied as he handed the reins to Thoralf.

He placed the basket on his lap, pausing for a second to ask me what I thought it was.

"It smells like cookies. Am I right?" I asked.

Thoralf and I tried to peak into the basket, but Onkel Tarald did a good job of blocking our view. He reached in and pulled out a biscuit.

"Well, your aunt has made us some fine-looking biscuits." he paused and looked in the basket. "Oh, what is this at the bottom?" He placed his hand back in the basket and stirred things around a little. "I know I saw something down here."

The waiting was killing me. I had to know what it was. What had Tante Anna made?

Onkel Tarald exclaimed, "There it is!" And pulled out three cookies.

He put one in his mouth, handed one to me, and then took the reins back from Thoralf and gave him the third one. Thoralf and I both said thank you with our mouths full of cookies. Tante Anna had made berliner kranser, a butter cookie in the shape of a wreath that we normally got only at Christmas time. It was a very special treat any other time of the year.

While eating the last of our snack, we reached the stacks of peat, and Onkel Tarald stopped the wagon. He jumped down, and we climbed into the back. He started handing the peat cakes up to us. We stacked them as fast as he handed them up. They did not smell now that they had dried.

As we finished loading each stack from the ground, Thoralf grabbed the reins and moved the horses forward to the next stack. Soon the cart was full, and Onkel Tarald climbed in and turned the horses around to head to Bestemor's house to unload. When we passed the house, Tante Anna was outside collecting the laundry that was hanging up to dry. Thoralf and I thanked her for the cookies, and just then Onkel Tarald said to look in the basket. He said that the biscuits and cookies that were left were for the whole family when we got home, but then he reached in the basket and pulled out three more cookies.

"Well, maybe not these," he said. "These three are for us." He put another cookie in his mouth with a smile. I laughed. Onkel Tarald liked cookies even more than I did.

November 30, 1936

As Thoralf and I approached the house on our way back from school, we saw a bicycle by the front steps that had baskets on the front and back. It wasn't ours. As we walked up the front stairs, the door was slightly ajar, and then a woman I had never seen before walked out the front door with a bucket.

She looked at us and said, "Boys, fill this bucket up and bring it inside. Hurry now!"

She handed Thoralf the bucket and went back inside before either of us could ask what it was for. Then we heard a scream. Thoralf and I looked at each other and ran to fill the bucket in record time. As I opened the door, Bestemor was standing there. She took the bucket and said, "Get your brother, Odd, and the three of you stay outside." There was another scream, and it sounded worse than the first one. "Go on, get outside, but don't wander off. We may need you to help."

"Help with what?" I asked.

"Your mother is in labor, and soon you will have a brother or sister," Bestemor said quickly. "Mrs. Salversen has come to help deliver the baby. If she needs anything else, I will let you know." she hurried back into the parlor, closing the door behind her.

Thoralf grabbed Odd, and we quickly went outside. I turned to Thoralf and said, "I am not sure what she meant by 'help,' but you are the oldest. I think if they need any help it should be you. I can watch Odd."

Thoralf replied, "Mrs. Salversen is here, silly. They are not going to need any help delivering the baby. Just help with getting things so they don't have to leave Mom alone. Remember when Odd was born? We sat outside with Dad while Mom and Mrs. Salversen, the person who lived near us, helped. Dad did most of the work, and I watched you."

I could not remember this, but Thoralf seemed confident that we would not have to do anything scary. That was reassuring. As we sat on the steps, we talked about wanting a sister. Even Odd said he wanted one when we asked him. As we waited, we took turns throwing small rocks at a larger rock we had placed on a stump.

The night wore on, it got darker outside, and Mom's cries became more frequent. Thoralf and I had gathered up some small wood and started a fire to keep us warm. Just as we started to warm up a bit, there was one more scream and then the sound of a crying baby. The baby cried only for a moment, and then we could hear Bestemor crying with excitement. She came to the door and told us we had a sister, a beautiful baby sister. She said we could come inside and sit in the kitchen, and she would get us something to eat soon. As I walked past the slightly opened door to the parlor, I could see Mom with a big smile on her face holding our new sister. I was not sure how after all of that screaming she could be smiling, but she was.

For the next few days, Mom slept downstairs in the parlor, and Odd slept with Bestemor so he would not be alone. After two weeks, we were all back upstairs, and with the exception of a crying baby waking us in the middle of the night, the sleeping routine was back to normal.

February 21, 1937

In February, Thoralf and I woke up to Odd screaming. Mom jumped out of bed and went over to him, saying that it was okay and that it was just a bad dream. Odd was left in bed alone because Bestemor was an early riser, and she let him sleep until Mom awoke. He was still getting used to being alone in bed now that he no longer slept with Mom.

"I can't move my legs! I can't move my legs!" Odd cried.

Mom looked frantic and said, "Thoralf, get dressed and go get the doctor and come back right away. Trygve, take Thelma downstairs and keep her warm. Tell Bestemor that Thoralf is going to get the doctor and that Odd cannot move his legs."

Thoralf pulled on his shirt as he ran out the bedroom door, and I quickly got dressed. I picked up Thelma, who was swaddled in a blanket Bestemor had made. Even with all that was going on, she was still asleep. When I picked her up, she made just a little sound, yawned, looked at me briefly, and fell back asleep. I rocked her gently and then carefully walked down the stairs and into the kitchen.

As I walked in, Bestemor asked, "What's all the commotion? Did Odd have another nightmare? And where is Thoralf running off to?"

"Mom sent Thoralf to get the doctor and told me to bring Thelma downstairs and tell you that Odd cannot move his legs."

Bestemor stopped what she was doing and stood frozen in front of the stove. After a moment she turned, walked out of the kitchen and into the guest room on the first floor. I followed her with a sleeping Thelma in my arms.

The guest room was a special place, reserved for friends and family when they visited. It was decorated with Bestemor's favorite things. She would occasionally go in there by herself or with Mom to sit and sew or knit. I think that Thelma, even at less than three months old, had been in there more than Thoralf, Odd, and me combined, but she'd been asleep for most of it. I had been in there only a few times, and never long enough to sit down.

Bestemor turned down the bed, moved things around, and dusted.

"Are you expecting company?" I asked.

"No, but if Odd has what I think he has, then he will be moving down here for a while," she replied.

Just then Thoralf came back in the door followed by Dr. Halversen. Bestemor told the doctor to go up the stairs and take the door on the right. Then she told Thoralf and me to go into the kitchen, and she would get us something to eat. We went into the kitchen and sat down. Bestemor put a loaf of bread on the table with a jar of blackberry jam. Thelma was now awake and crying as if she were hungry.

"I will take Thelma and get your mom to feed her while you eat," Bestemor said. "Stay in the kitchen until the doctor is gone." Then she walked into the parlor, rocking Thelma in her arms.

Thoralf took the bread and cut off two slices as I opened up the jam.

"I wonder what is wrong with Odd," I said.

"I think he has polio," Thoralf replied.

Just then Mom yelled down to us, "Thoralf, come upstairs! We need your help!"

Thoralf got up while putting the last bite of bread in his mouth and headed upstairs. I started to follow him, but Bestemor intercepted me and told me to stay down in the kitchen. A few moments later, the doctor and Thoralf carried Odd down the stairs and placed him in the bed in the guest room. Mom followed them quietly.

After the doctor talked to Mom a little more, he came out and gathered us all in the parlor. Mom stayed in the guest room with Odd.

"Odd has polio. For everyone's safety, you are all quarantined until further notice. I will tell Tarald what has happened." The doctor and Onkel Tarald were good friends.

Mom came out of the guest room and handed the doctor a note to give to Onkel Tarald. The doctor took the note and went out the door. A few seconds later, I heard a banging noise and looked out the window. He had nailed a sign on the tree that said, "Polio Quarantine."

Mom took Thelma from Bestemor and went into the kitchen to feed her. Bestemor looked at us for a second, deep in thought, and then said, "Okay, boys, it is time to clean up. Go outside and bring in two pails of water, take them upstairs, and fill the large kettle in the cellar so I can boil the sheets. Hurry up, get moving!"

"But the sign outside say that we are quarantined," I replied.

Bestemor said that we were allowed to go into the yard as long as there was no one else out there. This made sense because the only way to get water was from the well.

Thoralf and I spent all of that day cleaning things and boiling clothes. We scrubbed the walls and the floor of the bedroom and then the hallway and stairs. My hands were like prunes, all shriveled and soft. We were doing most of the work because Mom would not take Thelma into the room with Odd. If Mom was in there, then Bestemor was working while holding Thelma or sitting with her and knitting.

After lunch we washed down the kitchen, foyer, and parlor. I could hear Odd groan every now and then. I asked Bestemor if we would all get polio, and she quickly said, "No, not if we do a good job cleaning this house."

Thoralf and I scrubbed even harder to make sure we got everything clean. When I went outside to dump the dirty water and fill the pail again, I could see Onkel Tarald coming up the road. When he got to the tree stump on the side of the road just below our house, he stopped. He placed the basket he was carrying on the stump and yelled to me, "Here is a basket with dinner in it and some other small things. There is also an empty jar in here. Put a list of what you need in the jar, and place it in the basket and back on this stump. I or someone will come by every day to see what you need. Wait until I have left to come and get it." He then turned and headed back down.

I could see that he had left the wagon and horses down the hill a bit, where it would be easy to turn them around. When I saw him climb on the wagon, I walked over to the basket. Onkel Tarald waved. Then he turned the horses around and was soon out of sight. I missed the usual head rub he would give me as a hello and now wondered how long it would be before I would get another one.

Bestemor opened the door and asked what I was doing so far from the well. When I turned around, she could see that I had a basket in my hands, and she waved for me to bring it up to her.

As I came inside, she told me to place the basket on the kitchen table and finish helping Thoralf with the scrubbing. Thankfully, she said we were almost done. We soon finished cleaning and started to put back the furniture we had moved. Odd was now asleep, and Mom was sitting at the kitchen table. Thoralf and I sat on either side of her. She put her arms out and pulled us in, hugging us both at the same time.

"Odd will be fine," she said. "I will work with him every day to keep him moving, and he will be better in no time. The two of you will not be going to school for a while. I will send a letter to your teacher to have him send your schoolwork up, and Bestemor and I will teach you until you can go back."

Thoralf and I liked going to school and admired Mr. Dungvold, but we were sure Mom and Bestemor would be good teachers, too.

March 22, 1937

For the past several weeks, Thoralf and I had gotten up, completed our chores, and then did schoolwork. We both read a lot of books since there was now so much free time. My two favorites were *The Swiss Family Robinson* and *Treasure Island*. I read both of them twice just to make sure I did not miss anything. More than anything, I wanted to be on the sea and was sure that one day I would be a merchant marine like my Bestefar.

As the days got longer, we were allowed to go out into the yard and plant the garden. We were getting tired of being cooped up in the house, so being outside almost all day was wonderful.

June 17, 1937

A few more weeks went by, and then school was out for the summer. With no schoolwork to do, Thoralf and I were going stir-crazy. This was obvious to Bestemor, so after breakfast she took us into the cellar. She led us to a dark back corner that contained a pile of stuff covered with a dusty cloth and told us to look under it. Thoralf and I reached down and slowly pulled the cloth back. At first we saw field mice underneath. Bestemor was not afraid of them but was easily startled if one suddenly appeared and ran across her foot. When the cover was off, we found a pile of wood scraps of all different sizes and lengths. Bestemor pointed to a box in the corner.

"Go ahead, open it up," she said.

Thoralf and I slid it out. It was a tool box made of oak and stained dark on the outside. There was a long leather strap for a handle, attached at both ends. Thoralf wiped off the dust and opened it up. It was full of tools: saws, chisels, and two hammers—one small and one large. There was a hand drill with bits, screwdrivers, and a plane. There were so many tools in the box that I could not see the bottom of it.

Bestemor told us that this tool box had belonged to Bestefar. She said we were now old enough to use it but advised us to take good care of the tools because some of them had belonged to his father. She then pointed to the pile of wood scraps and told us that this wood was for us to use to build whatever we wanted. We both hugged Bestemor. It was very thoughtful of her to let us use Bestefar's tools.

Bestemor said, "Go on outside and build something, but stay right by the front steps."

Thoralf took the tools and I grabbed some of the wood and nails, and we ran out the cellar door into the front yard. Thoralf looked around and said, "We can use the front steps to cut the wood on."

He placed the box on the second step from the bottom, and I placed the wood on the bottom step. He opened the box and handed me a saw, and we started to work. Thoralf marked the wood, and I cut it. At first I was not even sure what we were making, but it was fun to be outside on such a nice day cutting wood with Bestefar's saw. Thoralf kept marking things, and I kept cutting. Some of the cuts were square, and others were at an angle. With several pieces cut, Thoralf started nailing them together. It quickly took shape, and I could see what Thoralf and I were making—a birdhouse! I grabbed the hand drill to make the hole. I cranked and cranked until the hole was finished. Thoralf nailed on the perch and then attached a piece of twine to the top of our creation. He ran to hang it from a tree in front of the house as I hurried inside to get Bestemor and show her what we had made. Bestemor liked songbirds, so we knew she would love having a birdhouse nearby filled with songbirds for her to listen to.

As I opened the door to escort Bestemor outside, a goldcrest flew by and landed on the perch of the newly constructed birdhouse. We quietly stood inside with the door half open to see what it would do. It poked its head through the hole I had drilled, and then it backed out and flew away.

Bestemor said, "What a beautiful birdhouse! I am sure it will have a resident soon." She gave us both a hug and told us to put the tools away, adding that we were now allowed to use them for things we needed to fix or wanted to build.

Just then, I thought about the loose plank at the edge of our bed. Grabbing the hammer and two nails, I headed upstairs to the bedroom. I stepped on the loose plank, pushing it down tight. Then I knelt down on one knee and nailed the loose floorboard to the floor joist. This would be the first of many things I tried to fix, some successfully and others maybe not so well.

August 1, 1938

This morning, I woke up to the smell of freshly baked bread. I sat up, took a deep breath, and noticed that I was the only person in the room. I jumped out of bed, quickly changed, and ran downstairs to find that Mom and Bestemor had gotten up early to bake. As I walked into the kitchen, Mom and Bestemor exclaimed, "Happy 9th Birthday!" And Odd joined in. He was sitting next to Thelma at the table, keeping her amused by playing with a small ball of dough. His fight with polio was over, leaving him with a slight limp. Thoralf came through the back door with the basket from the henhouse and handed it to Mom. "Happy Birthday, Trygve!" he shouted.

Mom thanked him and then turned to me and said, "Today for your birthday you are going to have eggs with warm bread and jam. Later, when you finish your chores—or at least the ones Thoralf has not already done for you—Onkel Tarald is coming by to take you and Thoralf fishing up on the lake." I ran to give Mom a hug and then thanked Thoralf for doing the chores. Odd said "Happy Birthday!" Again.

Mom told us all to sit down for breakfast. She pulled out two loaves of bread from the oven and placed them by the window to cool. Then she put the large black cast iron skillet on the stovetop, threw a little fat in it, and started cracking eggs. Bestemor pulled one loaf of bread from the window and started slicing it. I tapped my feet at a hundred miles an hour, excited about my birthday breakfast. The aroma in the kitchen was wonderful, and I could not imagine a better meal.

As she sliced the bread and gave some to each of us, Bestemor said, "If you catch enough fish, we can have them for dinner tonight."

Mom said, "Well, that is if my brother gets you home on time."

"Mom, Thoralf and I are good fishermen. We will catch plenty of fish long before dinnertime. We'll catch them so quickly that we will even have them cleaned before we get home," I replied.

Mom walked over and gave each of us a fried egg. Mine was just the way I liked it: sunny side up with a little bit of pepper on top. It looked perfect.

As we were eating, Bestemor walked over to the chair in the corner of the kitchen that held Bestefar's hat. She bent over and pulled out a small wooden box that I had not noticed before from under the chair. She turned with a tear in her eye and placed the box on the table.

"This was your Bestefar's fishing box," she started, her voice joyful. "He made this when he was a boy and used it when he went fishing with his father. You boys can use it today. Maybe it will bring you luck."

She picked up some of the dishes and brought them to the washbasin. Mom looked at the fishing box with amazement and told us that no one had used it since her father had died, not even Onkel Tarald.

"This is a great honor, and the two of you need to take very good care of it," she said softly.

"We will," I replied.

Thoralf slowly opened the box, and as he did, the hinges let out a slight creak. We looked at each other and then inside the box. There were assorted hooks, small weights, and some cork, each in little compartments on one side with some very weird-looking insects with hooks in them on the other. Mom could not resist looking inside either. She was now standing behind us, eyeing the box over our shoulders.

She explained, "See those flies in there? Bestefar would sit in his chair at the table during the long winters and make those. He would lose many over the summer to the fish but always had enough extras to fish the whole year."

Thoralf pulled out the top tray, placing it on the table to find another tray below it containing lots of different items for making flies. Under that tray were two knives in wooden sheaves and some fishing line. I had never seen so much stuff for fishing in one box.

Mom told us to get ready for Onkel Tarald. Thoralf took the box and placed it by the front door, and I went into the storeroom, grabbed a piece of burlap, and went outside to dig up some worms from the compost pile. I wanted to have them just in case the flies did not work.

As I came back inside, I grabbed a short piece of twine to tie up the burlap sack and walked into the kitchen. I was so anxious to go that I asked Mom if Thoralf and I could start walking down the hill to meet Onkel Tarald. She said yes, but to stop at Mr. Ellenes's store and wait on the front porch. If we did not see Onkel Tarald before then, we were not to go any farther.

I hugged Mom and scurried out the front door with my worms. As I ran by Thoralf sitting on the steps, I exclaimed, "Come on! Mom said we could go down the hill to meet Onkel Tarald!"

Thoralf grabbed Bestefar's fishing box, and down the hill we went. When we came to the fork in the road, we stopped running and started walking. We turned left to head up the hill and soon arrived at Mr. Ellenes's store.

Thoralf and I stood on the porch, not sure whether we could go in. I had been in his store only a few times and was curious to see what new things he had. The aroma of almonds gave me the courage to open the door. As I pushed it open, a rusty little bell attached to the door rang. Mr. Ellenes came out from the back and stood behind the counter.

"Hello, how are you boys today?" he asked, his voice pleasant. "What can I get you?"

"Today is my birthday, and Onkel Tarald is taking us fishing," I replied.

"Well, that seems like a good birthday present. I am sure he will be here soon. You should go back outside and sit on the bench and wait for him so he does not pass you by."

Thoralf and I turned and walked back outside to sit and wait. I was so fidgety that I could not sit down. I was ready to go fishing and needed to do something. I noticed a broom leaning against the barrel next to the bench. I put my burlap sack on the bench, grabbed the broom, and started sweeping the front porch.

After a few minutes, Thoralf pointed and said he could see Onkel Tarald coming down the hill. I kept sweeping. When Onkel Tarald pulled up, Thoralf ran to get into the wagon, and I quickly finished and put the broom back.

As I started to go down the stairs, Mr. Ellenes opened the door and said, "Where are you going? Come back here."

I turned and was not sure what I had done. Onkel Tarald said, "I see you put my nephew to work."

"I did not ask him to sweep the porch. He did it on his own," replied Mr. Ellenes. He waved me over and handed me two cookies with that wonderful almond smell. As he put them in my hand, he told me that when I started back to school in September, he could use someone to sweep the porch three days a week.

"If you do as good of a job as you did today, I can pay you. It won't be a lot, but maybe you will get the occasional cookie or two."

I thanked him and told him I would ask my mom about the job. I ate one of the cookies as I ran to the wagon. I jumped in and handed the other cookie to my brother and waved goodbye. Onkel Tarald nudged the horses, and we took off.

As we rode up the hill to the lake, Onkel Tarald glanced at the fishing box in Thoralf's hands.

"I see you have my father's fishing box. You must have been really good for my mom to give you that."

"Oh, she did not give it to us. She only lent it to us to bring us luck on Trygve's birthday," Thoralf explained.

"Well, that it will. My dad once caught a fish with just the hook and no bait. When I was very young, he was teaching me how to cast out and was adjusting the weight before he put the bait on. When he pulled it in, there was a fish on it. If I had not been there to see it, I would not have believed it. If it comes out of that box and gets tied to a fishing line, it is going to catch something," Onkel Tarald said with a laugh.

Thoralf and I looked at each other. Now we were sure this was going to be a good day to catch fish.

A short way up the hill from Mr. Ellenes's store, we turned left. This path was just big enough for the horses and cart, and we had to duck several times to avoid the branches from the birch trees.

After a few minutes we reached a clearing. I could see the shore of the lake just 200 feet away. There was a small rowboat turned upside down that looked as though it needed repair.

"There it is, boys. Valhalla," Onkel Tarald said with a hint of joy and wonder.

I could see that the word "Valhalla" was painted on the rear of the boat. Onkel Tarald stopped the cart, and we all hopped off. Thoralf chocked the wheels, and Onkel Tarald unhitched the horses, tied them to a tree, and gave them food and water. Thoralf and I went down to flip the boat over. Onkel Tarald brought down the oars and fishing gear, and the three of us pushed the boat a short distance across the rocky shore into the water. I was not sure it was going to float at first, but after we climbed in with all the gear, it was only leaking a little. Thoralf and I rowed as Onkel Tarald gave us directions.

Onkel Tarald prepared the fishing rods while occasionally bailing the water that was accumulating in the boat. When we were one-third of the way across the lake, he told us to stop rowing.

"This is the place, boys. We can start fishing and let the boat drift."

He handed each of us a rod rigged with a lure from Bestefar's box. I had never used anything so fancy. We cast out our rods in different directions at the same time, and the boat rocked from all the sudden movement. Soon we had our first bite. Thoralf jerked his line abruptly and wound it in, revealing a 16-inch trout. As he slung it into the boat, I grabbed it with both hands to remove the hook. I got the hook out but then dropped the fish into the boat. The water in the boat was now about four inches deep, and the trout quickly swam to the stern.

Onkel Tarald reached down and grabbed it. "Why, this is a very nice-looking fish you caught, Thoralf. We won't need many more of these for a good dinner."

Thoralf smiled as he cast his rod back into the water. A few minutes later, I had a fish on my line. I anxiously started winding the line in, but the fish must have changed direction, and the line went under the boat.

Onkel Tarald started to tell me to stop winding it in, but before he could get the words out, the line snapped. The bottom of the boat was rough and had cut the line. Onkel Tarald tried to console me by saying the line was old and that the fish was probably not very big, but I was sad that I had lost one of Bestefar's lures on my first try. Onkel Tarald handed me his rod and took mine to put a new hook on it. I told him that I would just use the worms that I had brought, but he insisted that I try one more of his father's lures.

The wind was starting to pick up slightly, and the boat was now drifting toward the shore. I am not sure if this had anything to do with what happened next, but suddenly we all had fish to reel in at the same time. None of the three we caught were any bigger than Thoralf's first catch, but they were still a good size, each about 14 inches long.

Onkel Tarald was now in charge of taking the fish off the hooks while Thoralf and I kept fishing. Our Onkel only had to bail the water from the boat one more time because the leaks had swelled back shut from being in the lake. Onkel Tarald took the oars and slowly guided the boat back toward our launch site. I caught three more trout, and Thoralf caught two more. When we returned to shore, Thoralf and I put the gear back on the hay cart while Onkel Tarald cleaned the fish. Then we dragged the boat back up the shore and flipped it over in the same spot we had found it in.

Thoralf and I helped hitch the horses to the cart, and we all climbed in. I had not noticed the changing weather while on the boat, but the clouds were now heavy and gray, and the wind was starting to blow a little more. Onkel Tarald said that it was soon going to rain and asked if we wanted to get wet. I was not sure why he asked us this strange question and replied that, no I didn't want to get wet. He then whipped the reins, and the horses started to trot. We were not headed back the way we came, but around the lake in the opposite direction. It was not long before we came to the top of a hill. Onkel Tarald stopped the horses and asked Thoralf and me to stand up on the bench.

"Can you see that rooftop?" he asked, pointing not into the woods but just over the treetops. "That house is Bestemor's house. If you take this path through the woods, it leads you to the open field just north of her house. It should only be a ten-minute walk from here. You can take the fish, and I will take all of the gear home and bring it to you another day."

With the wind now blowing steadily, I was not sure about this shortcut. Nonetheless, Thoralf and I did not want to look as if we were scared, so we jumped off the cart, took the fish, thanked Onkel Tarald for the outing, and started into the woods. The first part of the path was a little rocky, and we slid occasionally for the first hundred feet. The woods soon turned from birch trees to evergreens. The wind was now not as loud, but the rustling sounds of the branches and the falling sprigs from above made this path seem scary.

The scariness was short-lived, though, because the path soon opened up into the field just above Bestemor's house. We could now see the house and the stone wall just behind it. We could also feel the first few drops of rain. We began to run across the field.

Once near the house, we jumped up and over the short stone wall and went in the back door as the rain started to pick up. When we came out of the pantry and into the kitchen, Mom and Bestemor turned in their seats at the kitchen table, startled.

Mom took only a moment to figure things out. "I see my brother has shown you the short way home from the lake. I guess you were going to find out about it one day." she paused for a second and added, "It looks like you caught a lot of fish."

Thoralf and I were stunned that she was not mad, and we began to tell her about our day. Bestemor took the fish from us while Thoralf and I sat at the table. She cut some of the fish into strips to dry to eat another day, and the rest we had for dinner.

For me it was a perfect end to a great birthday.

September 4, 1939

Today at work, Mr. Ellenes was finally going to teach me how to bake bread. For all of the last year working for him, he had taught me only how to start the fire to warm the oven. I did this in the mornings on my way to school. I would stack logs in alternating directions in the large brick oven at the rear of the store. I placed dried pine cones at the bottom and in the middle of the stack, since they were easy to light. Mr. Ellenes would tend to the fire during the day, adding more wood and moving it around to heat the oven evenly. He had a real knack for that, and his breads were always golden brown and delicious. Today I learned that they did not turn out that way by chance.

"Trygve," he called to me as I entered the shop, "look in the oven and tell me what you see."

I looked in the oven and saw a layer of hot embers spread evenly on the bottom.

"Now," he said as I looked back at him, "take the lute and shovel. Pull out the embers and place them in the pail."

I was sweating from being so close to the oven and took off my shirt, leaving only my undershirt. After removing the embers, he told me to use the broom hanging from the side of the oven to sweep out the remnants of the fire.

"Okay, that looks good," he said when I was done. "Now take this mop and wet it in that pail of water, and wring it out. Then place this cloth around it, dunk it back into the water, and mop out the inside of the oven. Make sure to mop only the bottom, and spin it in your hand as you go from side to side. That will help clean the bricks on the bottom and keep the cloth from drying out."

I placed the mop in the pail and ended up with more water on the floor than on the cloth.

"Here, let me show you first, and then you can do it the next time." he took the mop from my hands. "You are doing a good job, but it is a lot to learn all at once."

He wrung out the cloth, wrapped it around the mop, dunked it quickly in and out of the pail, and put it into the oven, swabbing down the bricks with a nice, even-paced motion. There was steam and a sizzling sound as the water quickly evaporated.

"Isn't that going to cool off the oven?" I asked him.

"Yes, it is," he replied as he did it a second time. "We don't want the bottom of the bread to cook faster than the top because it may burn. I know the temperature of the bricks by looking at how fast the water evaporates, and it needs to be just right."

Mr. Ellenes made it look easy and moved to the next step, placing the bread in the oven. He removed the loaves from the racks where they were rising and placed them on the lightly floured bread peel.

"Now take the peel and place the loaves at the rear of the oven on the right side," he instructed. Evidently, there was a specific order to loading the oven. "You want to make sure that you are not reaching over things. Load the back-back-right-right and -left-left sides first, and then load the center so it is easy to pull the peel out. Then do the same in the front."

I gave the peel a quick jerk, and the loaves came right off, pretty close to where they needed to be. Mr. Ellenes looked over my shoulder, telling me not to move them if they were not exactly where they should be. It would become easier after I had more practice, he added.

With all 12 loaves now in the oven, he told me to get a drink. Loaves of this size needed to be moved four times about every six minutes. He told me to watch how he moved them around in a specific order and to always do it the same way so that each loaf would be in each quarter of the oven once, and they would all come out looking the same.

When it was time to make the first move, he had three peels and took two loaves out from the center, placing them on the peel on the oven apron to his right. Then he pulled out two more loaves, placing them on the peel on the oven apron to his left. He proceeded to move the remaining loaves around the oven in a clockwise direction and then placed the loaves on his left and right back into the oven. All of this took him less than 30 seconds, and at first I was not sure I could do it that fast, but by the time the loaves of bread were done baking, I was pretty good with the peel. With the first dozen loaves out of the oven, we were starting on the next dozen when the front doorbell rang. Mr. Ellenes and I walked to the door to find that my teacher, Mr. Dungvold, had come by to get his usual loaf of bread. He seemed very agitated, and he paced around the store.

"The Germans have invaded Poland," he said, walking back and forth in front of the counter. "This is not good. I think the Germans are going to try to take over Europe again. The Nazi party is a lot more organized than the German party was during the Great War."

Mr. Ellenes replied, "I would not be so worried about it right now. Let's see if they can even conquer Poland. So much of the Great War was fought in the trenches, and no one got very far."

"Maybe you're right, Christian," answered Mr. Dungvold, "but this Adolf Hitler seems to have his people brainwashed. I think he is a bad seed that was planted in the ruins of the Great War and has somehow sprouted and grown above all the others."

As they talked, Mr. Dungvold was steadily taking items off the shelves and placing them on the counter. Mr. Ellenes told me to go in the back and get a loaf of bread. He asked if Mr. Dungvold needed anything else.

"No," he replied, "that is all I need."

I placed the loaf of bread in a bag and handed it to Mr. Dungvold. He thanked me and turned to head out the door, saying, "I will keep listening to the radio and let you know what happens next, Christian."

After Mr. Dungvold left, I walked over to Mr. Ellenes and asked him who Adolf Hitler was.

"He is the leader of Germany. Over the past few years he has rebuilt the German economy from the ashes of the 1914 World War. I am afraid that Mr. Dungvold may be correct that this Hitler means to start another big war and that Poland is the first of his targets. We will know his true intentions by how the battle with Poland turns out."

I told Mr. Ellenes that Mr. Dungvold taught us about the Great War and about how many people died for very little land and that the Germans were defeated.

"Yes, they were," replied Mr. Ellenes, "but I think they may have learned from their mistakes. Let's get back to work. That bread is not going to bake itself."

October 12, 1939

In school, Mr. Dungvold added a new item to our schedule. Along with our history, arithmetic, grammar, and heritage studies, we would now be discussing current events. We had always talked about happenings in town, such as someone's new brother or sister, or a special day coming up, like May 17, the anniversary of Norway's independence from Denmark, but we would now also discuss the war in Europe. Mr. Dungvold started with the German invasion of Poland.

"The Germans have much better weapons than they had in the Great War, like much faster planes and tanks," he began. "They have moved through Poland like a knife through butter. I do not expect it will take them long to decide whom they will attack next. With the help of the Russians, they have divided Poland in half, and each country is now setting up the new government for its portion. Make sure to tell your parents about this when you get home."

For the remainder of the day, Mr. Dungvold commented on the Germans and Adolph Hitler in between our other studies. It was clear that something important was happening, and he wanted us to know.

December 17, 1939

Today when Thoralf came back from town, he was very excited. I was outside playing with Thelma in the remnants of the first snow, and Odd was sitting on the front steps throwing snowballs at the well. As Thoralf approached the house, he was pedaling the bike faster than I had ever seen him before. He was yelling something, but I could not make it out.

Odd said, "He is saying, 'You took my spot! You took my spot!' but I am not sitting in his spot."

When he pulled up in front of us he was winded, but he wore a big smile. He leaned the bike against the tree and exclaimed, "Look what I've got! Look what I've got!"

As Thoralf waved a letter in our faces, he darted between us up the stairs and through the front door. We followed him inside to see what was in the letter. When he got inside, Mom was sitting in the front parlor knitting with Bestemor.

"Mom, look what I've got! Look what I've got! It's a letter from Spangereid from Bestefar and Bestemor. Can you open it up and read it to us now?"

Mom put her knitting down and took the letter. We all gathered around and sat on the floor in front of her. Reaching into her sewing bag, she pulled out another knitting needle and used it to open the envelope, and then she began to read.

December 10, 1939

Dear Pauline, Thoralf, Trygve, Odd, and Thelma,

Pauline, thank you for your most recent letter. It is good to hear that Odd's fight with polio has left him with only a slight limp. He must really be getting tall by now. I miss my little buddy.

Thoralf and Trygve, I have not been fishing as much since the two of you left, but I do manage to row out once in a while and catch a fish or two. It is not the same though. Bestemor wants me to ask if you both have been writing in your journals. I assured her you were and that you would bring them whenever you visit. She cannot wait to hear about what you have been doing.

Thelma, we are both anxious to meet you. We have enclosed a picture of us with this letter for you to keep. I hope you will all be able to visit this summer when school is out. It would make us both very happy to see you all.

Bestefar

"Mom, can we go visit them?" I asked. "I would like to show Bestemor my journal so she can see what I have been doing."

"We may be able to go in August," she replied. "Let's see how things go this winter and spring and, if not, you can always put some of the stories from your journal in a letter and we can send them to her."

December 23, 1939

Today is Lillejulaften, the day before Christmas Eve. This is the day every year when we cut down our Christmas tree and bring it in the house to decorate.

Pop had a good steady job now in America and was able to send Mom some money. Soon, he would have enough money saved up to buy tickets for all of us to join him. Mom said that when school let out in the summer, we would all be going to the United States to live as a family again.

After breakfast we got dressed to go outside. Mom made sure we were dressed warm enough for the cold before we marched out the back door. Thoralf grabbed the ax, and we headed up the hill through knee-deep snow into the woods. It was cold, but the air was still. You could see your breath if you did not have a scarf over your mouth. The snow was a bit too deep for Thelma, and she and Mom fell a little behind. I waited a moment and knelt down to let Thelma climb on my back, and we continued up the hill. It was not a very long walk to the small clearing where we had cut the previous years' trees. This year Odd got to pick out the tree—that is, if Mom approved of it, of course. When it was our turn to pick, we all seemed to think the house was much bigger than it actually was. Mom would then remind us that we lived in a house, not a barn, and that the ceilings were not very tall.

Odd walked around looking at all the trees, unsure which one was his favorite. Then he pointed and ran with his arm extended to one by the edge of the clearing.

"That one! I like that one!" he said.

Thoralf turned and looked at Mom. She smiled and nodded. He walked over to the tree, and in just seven quick blows it fell. Quickly he trimmed it and then grabbed the bottom of the freshly cut tree, with Odd grabbing the narrow top, and they started back down the hill. Thelma walked over to me with her arms extended and smiled. I knelt down again, and as she climbed on my back, she kissed me on the cheek. I told her she is my favorite sister—since I only had one I figured I was safe.

When we reached the house, Thoralf had already made up the tree stand and attached it to the tree. He and Odd were standing with it outside, waiting for Mom to tell us where to put it in the parlor.

"You know where it goes. The same place we put it last year, in the opposite corner from the stove. We don't want it drying out too quickly," Mom said.

When we went inside, Bestemor had already moved the chair from the corner and was coming down the stairs with a small box of decorations. She sat down and handed each of us one decoration at a time to place on the tree. Thoralf and I were each given a small tin candleholder with a four-inch white candle that had never been lit. Bestemor had several of these, and since we were tall enough to reach the entire tree, she told us to space them out from top to bottom. She gave Odd a paper bell with foil on it. He liked all the shiny decorations. She then gave Thelma a julekurver, a small heart-shaped paper basket that I had made the year before. Thelma opened it up and then looked at Bestemor, wondering why there was nothing inside. Bestemor told her that if she was good, there would be something inside of everyone's julekurver on Christmas. Thelma smiled with her eyes opened wide. She handed me my julekurver and then turned and asked Bestemor where hers was. Bestemor had already pulled it out and was ready to hand it to her.

"Where should I put it on the tree so Santa can find it?" she asked, confused.

Odd said she should put it on the back of the tree. Bestemor quickly said not to listen to him and that Santa was about as tall as I was and to ask me. I looked at the now beautifully decorated tree, pausing a moment to enjoy it. Thelma tapped me on the leg and reached up to hand me her julekurver. I took it from her, saying, "I think it will look best next to mine. Santa has found mine every year, so he's sure to find yours, too," and hung it up.

We stayed in the parlor, admiring our tree and enjoying the aroma of a freshly cut spruce. Mom came in with some cups of warm milk. We each took one, and she said that she had a treat for us. Reaching into her apron, she retrieved a chocolate bar.

"Where did you get that?" I asked.

"I took a little of the money you and Thoralf made helping other farmers and bought it to share," Mom answered.

She broke it into six pieces and gave us each one. Thoralf put his into his warm milk and stirred it in as it melted. Each of us did the same. The warm milk now had a smooth chocolate taste. I drank it very slowly, savoring the sweetness. The room was quiet, with only the sound of Bestemor's knitting needles occasionally clinking together. This was the only time Mom did this for us. She was diligent about adding any extra money she could to the sums Pop sent her for our trip to America. Often, there was very little left after buying only the bare necessities.

Every harvest season, after doing our own gardens and helping Onkel Tarald and Onkel Sigvald with their farms, we would help other farmers with whatever they needed. This ranged from pitching hay to picking potatoes off the ground after the farmers had tilled them up. Thoralf and I were paid a little money for our work, while Mom and Bestemor always worked for food or a percent of the harvest. At the end of a long day working in the fields, Thoralf and I might each earn 50 cents and have two baskets of potatoes, carrots, or other vegetables to carry home for Mom and Bestemor's work. We always managed to have enough food to eat throughout the year, though by March it was mostly potatoes and bread, with the occasional fish we caught if the pond was not frozen and it was not too cold to go fishing. No matter what, none of us complained and were glad for what we had. I finished my cup while sitting in the parlor, enjoying everyone's company. It was a good day.

December 24, 1939

After the morning chores today, Thoralf and I were allowed to go skating with other kids on the small pond by the school. It was cold outside, and the wind was intermittent with an occasional strong gust. Mom had given us some rolls to share, along with one of the jars of strawberry jam she had gotten from Tante Anna. I packed the food in my sack, and Thoralf put the skates in his. We were bundled up tight and went outside to put on our skis. The race was on. Thoralf and I bound the skis to our shoes as quickly as we could. The skis were old, with many leather straps that had to be laced in a specific pattern around our shoes. The toes and balls of our feet had to remain firmly in place while allowing our heels to rise up for the level and uphill portions of the cross-country journey. We were both skilled at fastening our skis, but it still took time, and Thoralf finished first.

"I am going to beat you there," he said as he started down the hill.

I finished with my bindings and was only a few seconds behind him. Thoralf was just past the neighbor's house where the long slow curve in the road began. He entered the turn and looked to see where I was. I was just passing our well, but he was still pushing ahead. As I approached the neighbor's house, I remembered the story Onkel Tarald told us about Mom and Tante Agny. I turned to go behind the house, hoping that the shorter distance and extra speed from the steeper slope would put me in the lead at the bottom of the hill. Luckily for me, the wind had blown the snow and piled it up against and over the short stone wall dividing the yards, allowing me to cross it with ease.

As I approached the woods, I couldn't see a clear path through them. The snow was loose, and the wind had kicked up some powder, impairing visibility. Not wanting to lose, I picked what I believed to be the correct path and headed into the woods. I held my poles up in front of me, using them to take the brunt of the impact from the low branches. Once in the woods, there were only a few low branches to contend with, but the snow was not as thick. The hill was now steeper, and I was skiing very quickly. This path seemed to have a lot more trees than I was told, and there was dead wood on the ground that was not completely covered by the snow. It required all my concentration not to get my skis caught on something.

With the clearing near the bottom of the hill now in sight, the tree branches started to thicken up again, and I put my poles in front of my face to soften their blows. Suddenly I felt my hat get yanked off my head. I reached up to grab it. With my head turned looking for my hat, I hit a large branch that was sticking out of the snow. Now off balance, I must have tumbled down the hill, because all I can remember is Thoralf standing over me asking me if I was okay.

"I knew you were going to try that shortcut," Thoralf said. "And I waited to see how it was going to turn out. When I got to the bottom of the hill and did not see you, I got worried, so I started up toward the trees, just in time to see you come flying out from the woods head first and into this big snow drift. Lucky for you."

"I am not sure how lucky I am—my shin is killing me, and I lost my hat," I replied.

"I can see your hat hanging from that branch, but what about the rolls and the jam in your bag?" Thoralf asked.

I opened the bag to see that some of the rolls were now flat, but they had cushioned the jar of jam, and it was not broken. Thoralf helped me up and brushed me off. Then he skied to the edge of the woods and reached in with his pole to dislodge my hat from the limb.

"Are you okay to continue?" he asked, handing me my hat.

"Yes, I will be fine. We are not going to tell Mom about this, are we? And maybe we should not tell Onkel Tarald either," I said with the occasional ouch between my words.

"Nope, we are not!" Thoralf chuckled. "But you are going to owe me one."

December 25, 1939

When I woke up on Christmas morning, I knew it was going to be a good day to relax. Since the quarantine a couple of years ago, there had hardly been any days when we all just stayed home and did what we wanted. Christmas was the one day of the year that we did very few chores, did not visit with anyone, or have anyone visit us. I am not sure why it had always been like this, but I liked it this way. I knew there would be lefse for breakfast with rice pudding. Mom would put one almond in the pot, and whoever was fortunate enough to get the almond in their bowl would have good luck all year. I knew there would be cod for dinner. Even if we hadn't had fish for days, Mom always saved some dried cod for Christmas dinner. With it there would be potatoes and carrots. Best of all, Bestemor would make her white onion gravy. Even as I lay in bed waiting for everyone to wake up, I could smell the meal to come. I just knew it was going to be a good day.

As I thought about the day ahead, I fell back asleep and was soon awakened by Thelma. "Wake up! Wake up!" she said, rocking me back and forth.

"Why should I wake up? Is there something I am missing? Am I late for school?" I joked, smiling.

"It's Christmas, and there are things under the tree for all of us!" she replied while dragging me out of bed. "Come on! You and Thoralf are the only ones we are waiting for."

Thoralf rolled over and said, "I thought my present was getting to sleep in today and that you and Odd were doing my chores."

Thelma hurried us down the stairs, talking the whole way.

"Come on, hurry up, look! There are presents under the tree. There are presents for all of us. I can see my julekurver has something in it. Yours has something in it, too. You were right! You put mine next to yours, and now they both have cookies in them!"

Mom had to calm Thelma down to start giving out the presents. Thoralf and I knew most of the things we would be getting because we had watched Mom and Bestemor knit them. Odd, I think, was just starting to catch on, but not Thelma.

Mom handed each of us a present wrapped in plain brown paper. Odd had managed to get his open first and held up a light grey scarf with three red stripes at each end. He started to thank Mom but bit his tongue. Next, we each opened up hats and mittens that matched our scarves. Thelma was trying on each item as she unwrapped it. There were now only a few presents left under the tree. Thoralf and I would always get a book. Mr. Dungvold had talked about *Moby Dick* in school a few weeks ago, and I had mentioned it several times during our dinner conversations but was not sure if Mom got the hint.

Thoralf opened his last present, and it was a copy of *20,000 Leagues Under the Sea.* Mr. Dungvold had also recommended this book to the class and said it was one of his favorites. Thoralf and I always shared our books, so I knew that when he was finished reading it, I would get it next.

When Mom handed me my last gift, I could feel a book through the wrapping paper. When I opened it, it was not what I had hinted for, but something even better—a book on stamp collecting.

"This is perfect!" I told Mom.

Thoralf, Odd, and I had each been taking turns carefully removing the stamps from the letters Mom and Bestemor received. We often fought over the ones from other countries, especially the ones from Pop. Thoralf and Odd looked over my shoulder as I flipped through the book, anxious to see the pictures and descriptions inside.

Finally, there were only three gifts left under the tree. Mom grabbed one and handed it to Thelma. It was a small box with an even smaller box tied on top. Mom told her to open the bigger one first. Thelma, now with her mittens off, managed to open it before Mom finished her instructions. It was a very nice new dress. Thelma held it up to show us and could not wait to put it on. Then she remembered that there was still a small present to be opened and quickly folded the dress up and placed it back in its box. She opened the smaller box and pulled out a very small dress made of the same fabric as the larger one.

Odd looked at it and said, "Mom, I think that one shrunk in the wash."

Thoralf and I laughed.

"That is for her doll so they have matching dresses," Mom explained.

Thelma grabbed her doll and put the new dress on her.

With only two presents remaining, Thoralf asked if he could give them out. Thoralf, Odd, and I had pooled our money to buy Mom and Bestemor each a present. Last year we noticed that they hadn't received anything, and we did not want that to happen again. Thoralf handed them each a gift, and they stared at each other, not knowing what to say.

"Go ahead, open them," I said.

Bestemor opened hers first, pausing only for a second and then holding it up for all to see.

"This is great! Parcheesi—I have heard of this game but have never seen one."

"It is a game originally from India. We learned about games from different countries in school," Thoralf explained.

"Well, we will all have to play it today. Thank you all very much," Bestemor replied.

Bestemor liked to play games with us. I think before we came to live with her, all she did was knit and sew and chores. She did not have time to play games and had no one to play them with. This was a good gift for her.

Mom had been sitting patiently with her gift in her lap while Bestemor opened hers. She smiled in anticipation and started to unwrap it. As she opened the box and started to pull the gift out, her eyes opened wide. I think she may have been crying, but I'm not sure. She held it up in front of her and smiled more than I had seen her smile in a long time.

"This is beautiful! Oh my, it is so beautiful!" Mom said as she placed it in her lap. She removed the lid by the half bobbin handle to look inside. "This is perfect. There are places for my needles and threads. There is even a place for my buttons. Thank you all! This is the nicest sewing box I have ever seen!"

The three of us smiled at each other—it was the perfect gift.

March 25, 1940

Every month, Pop wrote to tell us how things were going for him. Today's letter discussed the people he met and worked with. He was currently living in Brooklyn, New York, in a small room of a boarding house. He liked to work with wood and had a job with the Coughlan Flooring Company as a carpenter. When we were growing up, Pop was always constructing something, and he would let Thoralf and me help. He taught us how to use his tools.

We always remembered that he had told us, before he left for the United States, that we were in charge of helping Mom and that we needed to do what he would do while he was gone, since we were now the men in the family. In his most recent letter, Pop told us that he and his friends were helping a widowed woman with her problems. We were all happy to hear this. Mom paused from reading the letter out loud for a second and then folded it and put it in her apron.

Mom looked up. "Let's surprise your father by putting a picture of the four of you in our next letter. That way he can show his friends what lovely children he has."

We were excited about this idea, and I asked if I could add my own letter. Mom suggested that we each write a letter or draw a picture to send with hers, adding that we should start on it now, while Pop's letter was still fresh in our minds.

We went into the kitchen and sat at the table. Thoralf and I each wrote letters, while Odd drew a picture of himself catching a big fish at the lake, and Mom helped Thelma draw some pretty flowers. I am not sure what Thoralf wrote about; he did not share it with me. I wrote that Thoralf and I were doing exactly what he had asked us to do before he left and that we were doing almost as good a job as he would if he were here. Oh, and that Onkel Tarald had promised to take us fishing on the North Sea someday, but not to mention it in his next letter back to us. Mom did not think we were old enough to go out on the North Sea to fish and would only let Onkel Tarald take us on the lakes and ponds. I was sure Pop would keep my secret.

March 13, 1940

Dear Family,

I write to you today to wish Thoralf a happy 12th birthday. I miss you all more each day than the last, and I have been working as many hours as they will let me to save up the money needed for your passage to America. I have recently moved into a boarding house in Brooklyn. It is run by Mrs. Tharaldsen. She is from Oslo and is now living alone since the passing of her husband two weeks ago. I worked with her husband along with Mr. Haug and Mr. Tollison. The three of us are now renting rooms in her house to help her through the hard times. She is so grateful that she packs us lunch in the mornings to take with us when we leave for work.

Thoralf, Happy Birthday. I am sure you are as tall as me now, and I cannot wait to see how you have grown. You and Trygve remember what I told you.

Trygve, I hope today you have done all of Thoralf's chores as I am sure he did on your birthday. The best gift to give someone is free time to do what they want to do.

Odd, Mom tells me that you have been eager to help out and want chores of your own. This is great to hear and makes me proud.

Thelma, I can only dream of the day that I first get to meet you in person. I am sorry I missed another one of your birthdays. I am sure you are as pretty as your mother. Make sure to listen and learn all that you can from her and her mother. They are two very smart women.

Pauline, please do not read this portion out loud, as I want it to be a surprise. Mr. Haug has agreed to lend me some money to move you all here as soon as possible. Let me know how much you have from what you have saved and what I have sent so I only borrow what we need. I would appreciate it if you could send me a recent picture of the children to share with him.

Your husband,

Olaf

March 26, 1940

This afternoon Mom put us in our best clothes and walked us over to the neighbor's house. Mr. Mikalsen would be taking our picture with his new camera in exchange for some eggs. Thoralf, Odd, and I wore white shirts and white pants with gray woolen vests Mom had knitted. Thoralf's was new this past Christmas, while I wore his old vest, and Odd wore my old one. Thelma was wearing the red sweater Bestemor had knitted for her third birthday with a red hat, white stockings, and a white skirt.

Mr. Mikalsen set up his camera on a tripod. He lined the four of us up in front of some bushes next to his house. Thelma was not being very cooperative, and Mr. Mikalsen tried to get her to smile.

"This picture is for your father," he said. "You want to look your best for him, don't you? I know, how about I tell you a joke? What do you call a sad strawberry? A blueberry."

Thelma did not think this was funny and moved to hide behind Thoralf, but Odd laughed out loud, and I started to laugh at him. Mr. Mikalsen said to smile, and I heard the click of the camera and the picture was taken. I wondered what it was going to look like, but I was sure Pop would love it no matter what.

April 2, 1940

Mom went back to Mr. Mikalsen's to pick up the photo and gave him some dried fish for taking and developing the photograph so quickly. She showed it to us in the evening after dinner. It was not perfect, but Mom said it was very nice.

"Your father is going to be surprised and happy to get a letter from each of you along with this photograph," she said. "And I have a surprise—your father will soon have all the money we need for our trip to America."

At first I was happy to hear the news, but as I thought about it, I became sad. I could not wait to see my dad again, but who would help Bestemor when we left? Mom said that Bestemor could take care of herself and had done so for many years with the help of Onkel Tarald before we moved in, adding that her sister lived nearby, too. She then told us to go to bed because tomorrow, if we did all our chores, Onkel Tarald would take us fishing in the afternoon. Thoralf and I ran off to bed, excited and hoping that morning would come quickly.

April 3, 1940

Thoralf and I woke up early and started our chores right away. We both brought in wood for the stove, and then Thoralf fed the chickens and I cleaned up after them. I am not sure why Thoralf got to feed them and gather the eggs to take to Bestemor, and I had the smelly job of cleaning up. He said that it had been his job to clean up after the chickens, but when I turned six it became my job. As he explained this, I began to wonder why Odd wasn't doing this since he was now six. I decided to let Mom know that it was time Odd started doing some of these chores.

We flew through our chores and finished them all by lunchtime. As we sat inside eating, I told Mom that Odd was six and that he was now old enough to be cleaning up after the chickens, and I could do more important things. After thinking for a second, she replied, "You're right. Make sure to teach him how to do it the right way." I turned my head and smiled at Odd while eating my sandwich.

Thoralf and I finished our lunch and asked Mom if there was anything else we needed to do. She said, "No, you have done all the extra chores I have given you. You can get your poles and go fishing with Onkel

Tarald. He told me he would be in town today and had a surprise place to take you this afternoon."

We asked if we could be excused. Mom smiled and said, "Yes."

We jumped up, grabbed our fishing poles, and started to head out the door when Mom said, "Don't forget your brother." I was confused as I stared at Thoralf, who was standing right next to me.

"No, not him, your brother Odd," she clarified. "He is six now, and he gets to go fishing with the two of you."

Thoralf and I looked at each other and then grabbed our younger brother and headed out the door. If Mom said to do something, you did it. There was no arguing with her.

As we walked down the hill, we noticed that there were still patches of snow along the side of the road. Thoralf told Odd that he would have to row the boat because we only had two fishing poles, but it was an honor to row the boat—if he did a good job, the next time he went fishing, we would share our fishing poles with him.

Odd was just happy to be going with us. "Okay!"

As we got to the church just outside of town, I told Thoralf and Odd I would catch up with them because I wanted to check on Bestefar's grave. Thoralf said he would go with me, but Odd was uncertain about walking through a graveyard and said he would wait by the road. "We will be quick," I replied.

As we walked down the path to the front of the church and approached the headstone of the grandfather I had never met, I could see the snow still covering the hole

SAFL
SIDEWALK ADVOCATES
   FOR LIFE

LOVE   NO
COMPASSION   JUDGEMENT

   SHADOWING ON A
        FRI   AM

Groupmeap
   DESIRE FOR HOPE

      FB PASSWORD
CAPS GLELFR4161
     ~~490~~ 790594

To _____   **Date** _____

☐ SIGNATURE   ☐ INFORMATION   ☐ FILE

☐ ACTION   ☐ RETURN TO SENDER

☐ COMMENTS   ☐ PLEASE SEE ME

Remarks:

FRED KRUEGER
INDUSTRIAL ENGINES

where I would soon plant the begonias we had grown on the windowsill in the parlor. Thoralf helped me clear the snow so that the ground would thaw quicker. I thanked Bestefar for letting us use his fishing box and tools and told him that we had both made a birdhouse to hang by the front door. Thoralf added that the fishing box had brought us good luck and that we had caught a lot of fish using the tackle inside.

After a few more minutes, Thoralf and I headed back to get Odd. As we reached the street, Odd pointed ahead and said, "I see Onkel Tarald. There he is."

Onkel Tarald was leaning up against a small wooden fence talking to someone. The three of us ran over to meet him. I got there first and grabbed him around the waist and gave him a hug. Thoralf and then Odd soon joined me. We all hugged Onkel Tarald as the man standing next to him said, "I see you have a following there, Tarald. How did you get so popular?"

"Well, I see I have all my nephews today," Onkel Tarald said in his customary cheerful tone. "Good thing I brought an extra fishing pole with me." He added, "Boys, this is Mr. Jaartag. He owns the furniture factory just outside of Farsund and is lending us his boat to go fishing today. Mr. Jaartag, these are my nephews, Thoralf, Trygve, and Odd."

The three of us said hello, shook his hand, and thanked him for letting us use his boat.

I said to Mr. Jaartag, "My father wrote to us and said that we would all be going to the United States to live with him soon."

Mr. Jaartag replied, "That sounds like a great adventure. I have some relatives who moved to Brooklyn, New York, a few years ago and they live in the Norwegian part of town there."

"That is where our father is!" I replied.

"Well, maybe they know each other," Mr. Jaartag chuckled.

Onkel Tarald thanked Mr. Jaartag while shaking his hand and said we needed to get started before it got too late. Pointing at the boat in the small protected cove off the North Sea, Onkel Tarald said, "That is the boat. Take your stuff, and we will launch as soon as you get your things stowed."

I could see the boat at the end of a short wooden pier just 200 yards away. It looked huge—at least twenty-five feet long! Today no one would have to row. It was an all-wooden boat with a small cabin. The hull and cabin were painted white. As I approach the boat, I could see the name "Nerthus" on the stern, flanked on both sides by a Norwegian flag. I asked Onkel Tarald what Nerthus meant.

"Nerthus is the goddess of peace and fertility," Onkel Tarald explained. "Mr. Jaartag chose it after the birth of his eighth child, hoping that when he used it he would have some peace." Onkel Tarald laughed. "I am not sure things are working out like he planned, though."

He then instructed Thoralf and me to stow the gear and grab the lines to prepare to cast off as he started the engine. He picked up Odd, placed him in the boat, and climbed in behind him. They both went into the small pilothouse, and moments later I heard the engine. It sputtered a few times and spit out some black smoke but was soon running well. Onkel Tarald opened the rear door to the pilothouse and asked us to climb aboard to push the boat away from the pier. We jumped in the back of the boat. Thoralf grabbed a gaff and used it to push the boat away from the pier as I coiled up the lines. Onkel Tarald gave the engine some power, and we left the shore.

Thoralf and I then joined them in the pilothouse. It contained lots of dials and gauges. The teak wood that lined the walls resembled fine furniture. It was very shiny and smooth to the touch. The water in the protected cove looked like glass, and the boat glided through it much like a skater on ice. As we gazed out into the North Sea, we saw that it, too, was very calm. Onkel Tarald was not going very fast, and as other boats passed us, we waved to them, and the people on them waved back. This was all very exciting to me.

About a half mile off shore, Onkel Tarald slowed the boat. He instructed us to bait the rods, cast them out, and then place them in the rod holders at the stern. He and Odd had piloted the boat to a spot where the warmer water was known to be heavy with fish. Norway is known for its ice-free ports in the winter. This is because the Gulf Stream begins its long journey off the coast of Florida and goes up the east coast of the United States and across the Atlantic Ocean before ending up on the west coast of Norway.

As we approached this spot, one of the rods had a bite and began to bend. Onkel Tarald came out of the pilothouse. He locked the wheel in a slow turn to the port and then latched the pilothouse door open. Odd's line moved quickly, first away from and then back under the boat. He smiled widely because he had never been the first to catch a fish before, and this was his chance to one-up his older brothers.

Thoralf said, "Are you going to pull him in or let him get away?"

Odd replied, "I want to make sure the hook is in all the way."

He jerked the line one time and wound it in. It was a mackerel, about 11 inches long. Onkel Tarald grabbed the fish, took it off the hook, and put it in the barrel.

As Odd was rebaiting his line, Thoralf and I each had nibbles on ours and hooked two more fish. We did not play with them as long as Odd had. We quickly pulled them into the boat, and Onkel Tarald unhooked them and put them in the barrel. Now as fast as we could bait the hooks and put them back in the water, we were catching fish, all mackerel 10 to 12 inches in length. We continued for almost 30 minutes. We had so many fish that Onkel Tarald stopped fishing because the barrel was almost full. A few minutes later, the fish stopped biting, and the lines went limp. I turned around to see that we were now heading toward the Lista Lighthouse.

"Where are we going, Onkel Tarald?" I asked. "The fish were really biting where we just were."

"We have enough mackerel and have almost run out of space to put any more in. So I have decided to take you all to see the lighthouse from the water. You have only ever seen it while on land," he replied.

We were now moving at a quicker pace, and even with the calm water, there was the occasional bow spray misting back on us. We moved into the pilothouse with Onkel Tarald to stay dry. As we approached the lighthouse, I noticed a German fishing boat. German boats had often come to this part of the North Sea this time of year to fish, but they were a lot closer to the shore than usual. There were men at the bow and stern of the boat casting off lines and then pulling them back up, but there weren't any fish hooked. Onkel Tarald noticed this too and slowed our boat down. He looked a little concerned and directed us to put our lines back in the water, saying, "We are in a better spot than the Germans, so our lines won't be coming up empty." We put our lines in, and Onkel Tarald slowly turned the boat around, getting closer to the German fishing boat.

"Onkel Tarald, I thought we didn't have any room for more fish?" Thoralf asked.

"If the German fishing boat thinks this is a good spot, then there might be cod here to catch," he replied.

Onkel Tarald had been fishing here for more than 30 years and knew where the fish would be, so we listened. I noticed he kept looking over his shoulder at the Germans' boat and seemed more interested in what they were doing than fishing with us.

We fished for only about five minutes before Onkel Tarald told us to bring the lines in, stow the gear, and come into the pilothouse with him because it was time to head back. Onkel Tarald let each of us pilot the boat for a few minutes to see how it handled. Odd was so excited when it was his turn that he kept over-correcting, and the path back was more like a zigzag than a straight line.

While we were making our way back, the German fishing boat had moved farther up the coast, but I could still see it off in the distance as we turned to head into the cove. I asked Onkel Tarald why we were catching so many fish and the Germans were not. He replied that they were after a different type of fish and then quickly told Odd to hold on as our boat began rocking side to side from the wake of a passing boat. "Your mom won't let me take you fishing again if I bring one of you back wet!" he said.

Once back at the pier, we unloaded the boat and thanked Onkel Tarald for the best boat ride and fishing trip we had ever had. He said that he had a good time, too, and that we could take the fish home with us. I asked him why he did not want any and he responded, "I need to go into town to talk to a friend, and the fish need to be cleaned right away, so hurry home with them."

We thanked him again and headed for home, each with a burlap bag full of fish on our backs. As we walked up to the house, Thelma was outside with her friend, Signy. Thelma ran to meet us, asking if we had caught any fish. Odd said that he caught the first fish and it was the biggest of them all. Thoralf and I were quick to say that we each had caught the most, even if they weren't the biggest; we did not want to be bested by our younger brother. After all, it was his first time out in a boat. He had been fishing only on the shoreline at the nearby lake before today and always played more than fished. I explained that his success must have been because Thoralf baited the rod Onkel Tarald had brought for him to use.

"Yes," Thoralf agreed, "that had to be the reason. Next time we will make Odd bait his own line."

As we made it to the front door, Mom and Bestemor came outside to get the fish so they could clean them. Odd again had to say that he caught the first fish and that it was the biggest one of all. When she saw our bags, Mom said, "Look at all these fish! Did the three of you catch all of them?"

We all replied "yes" at the same time.

"This is wonderful!" she said. "We will have fish for dinner, and we can dry the rest to eat another day."

She told Thoralf to get some more wood for the stove and me to go into the root cellar for potatoes and rutabaga. Thelma, who had snuck up behind me, said, "Yuck. I don't like rutabaga."

Thoralf and I did as we were asked, plus a few other chores. Soon, Mom called us all in and said it was time to eat. We ran inside and sat at the table. Mom said grace and added in a special line for her three sons who had done such a great job providing for the family. "Amen," she concluded.

Mom had cleaned the fish and fried it in a little fat. It looked great! Bestemor had taken the potatoes and the rutabaga and boiled them and mashed them together. We all dug in and soon cleaned our plates—even Thelma. Maybe she hadn't noticed that the rutabaga she hated so much was mixed in with the potatoes, or perhaps she was just so hungry that she did not care. Either way, we were soon stuffed.

I later learned that, as we walked home, Onkel Tarald was making a stop of his own.

When we parted ways, he hurriedly headed toward town to see his friend, Dr. Halversen. When he arrived, he knocked on the door. "Lars, it's me, Tarald, open up."

Dr. Halversen opened the door. "Are you okay? Is someone sick?"

"Yes, I have cut myself and need you to look at it," Onkel Tarald replied.

Dr. Halversen let him in. "Here, sit in this chair. Let me get a bandage and something to clean your cut with..." he paused as he looked at Onkel Tarald. "Well, where is it?" he asked.

"I am not cut, but I have something to tell you and do not need anyone else hearing this right now," explained Onkel Tarald. "I have just come from fishing and saw one of the German fishing boats sounding for depth all along the coastline. What do you think this means?"

Dr. Halversen thought for a moment. "Are you sure that is what they were doing? Norway is neutral."

"I saw what I saw," he answered.

Then Dr. Halversen said, "This cannot be good. I always thought the British would mine the channel to stop the German navy from getting through the straits. If they have, then the Germans' only hope is to navigate close to our shores, but sounding is more for submarines than ships. Let me talk to someone I can trust in Farsund, and I will let you know what they say. Tell no one about this."

Dr. Halversen then put a bandage on Onkel Tarald's arm and said, "This is in case someone was listening when you came in."

Onkel Tarald nodded and left.

April 6, 1940

Tante Agny came to stay with us for a few days. After breakfast, we all went up into the storage side of the attic directly across from our bedroom. It's a place I went only when Bestemor needed help with something. Its wooden plank floor was not as nice as the rest of the floors upstairs, and you could see the underside of the roof when you looked up. There was a window just like the one in our bedroom, but without any trim on it, and the walls did not have plaster on them. There was a good layer of dust on everything in the room.

When we reached the top of the steps, Bestemor told us to follow her all the way into the back near the window. There she pulled a tarp off an oddly shaped item, slowly so as not to stir the dust into the air. She folded the tarp and handed it to Odd to take outside, telling him to hang it up and beat the dust off. With the tarp off, I still wasn't sure what I was looking at and thought it might be in pieces. In the pile I saw a frame that had two foot pedals and another with arms and braces.

Bestemor told us the order in which to bring the pieces downstairs to the parlor. As we did, Mom and Tante Agny started to assemble the parts. Even when it was finished, I was still not sure what it was. Thelma spoke up. "What is this thing?"

Agny answered, "See that carpet runner on the floor in the hallway outside this room? Your mom and I made that when we were younger with this loom."

"Younger like me?" Thelma asked.

"Well, maybe not that young, but watch us, and one day when you are a little older, you can make one yourself."

With the loom put together, Agny asked Thoralf and me to follow her into the guest room. On the floor were two large bags full of cloth scraps. We each dragged one of them into the parlor. Mom and Tante Agny began to sort the scraps and cut them into strips about three inches wide. Bestemor had now finished adjusting the loom and began setting the main yarns, which she called the warp. This looked very complicated to me. There were so many yarns to thread through the loom, and I just stared as Bestemor made quick work of it. Mom put many of the scraps together and wound them on an oddly shaped stick with notches at each end. She handed it to Bestemor, and the weaving began. They continued for hours.

Thoralf and I packed some food and took Odd up the hill to sit and look out over the sea we had been fishing in just a few days earlier. I had a new appreciation for this view, having been out there. I could see fishing vessels close to shore and other types of ships off in the distance. I wondered whether they were war ships or just transport ships; at their current distance I could not tell. There had been a definite increase in the number of ships visible from this hilltop since the start of the war, though.

After eating, we chased each other playing tag, and then we tried our skills at throwing small rocks at other small rocks we had placed on the top of a stump. We did this until it was almost dark. When we returned home, Mom and Bestemor were still in the parlor talking and weaving. There was a very colorful rug about ten feet long laid out on the floor, and Tante Agny was working on another one. The three of us said goodnight and went up to bed. We left Thelma sleeping on Bestemor's lap and Mom and Tante Agny weaving and chatting.

PART 2

April 9, 1940

Thoralf and I were walking to get milk from Onkel Sigvald and Tante Palma's farm. Tante Palma is Mom's younger sister. Their cow had just had its first calf, and it was now weaned off of its mother's milk, so they offered us the extra milk they had. They lived a little more than three kilometers from us, just past the schoolhouse but far off the road. They had a lot of sheep, two cows, the new calf, and large pastures for them to graze in. At one point, they also had a few chickens, but something got to them, and now there were none. I am sure this is why we kept our chickens inside and let them out only during the day in the small fenced-in area, when the weather permitted. Mom said we would let some of our eggs hatch and bring them the chicks so they could have eggs of their own again. In the meantime, we brought them eggs. Mom did not like being given anything without giving something in return, so now, with their lack of chickens, we always had something to exchange for milk.

As we approached the house, Tante Palma was outside hanging up the laundry with her newborn son, Svein, lying in a small bassinet next to her. Their house was very similar to Bestemor's. In fact, most of the houses around us in the mountains were about the same—white houses with wooden siding and not a lot of trim. The houses were built on top of a stone cellar, and some had barns. A few, like Onkel Tarald's, were a little larger and fancier.

When she saw us approaching, Tante Palma said, "Hello, boys. How are the two of you today?"

We both said we were doing well. Thoralf was holding a basket with a few eggs in it, and I had two empty milk jugs. Thoralf handed her the basket, and I asked where Onkel Sigvald was.

"He is in the fields tending to the sheep with the two older ones," she replied. "Here, come with me to the barn so you can milk the cows. And thank you for bringing me these eggs."

We walked around the yard and into the barn. Gertie and Emma were in their stalls, and the newborn calf was asleep, tied to a post. Tante Palma showed us where the milking pails and stools were and said she would be inside with Svein if we needed her.

"Let me know when you are done. I may have a surprise for you when you leave for the walk home," she said, entering the house.

I took a big sniff to see if I could guess what it might be, but I could only smell the cows.

Thoralf and I got to work right away. He took Emma to milk, and I had Gertie. First we moved the cows forward, putting their heads through the gate at the feed trough, and then we closed the gate down until they could not back up but could still move their heads freely. We washed the udders and our hands and began to milk them. At first the sound was a tiny "ting" as the milk hit the empty metal pails, but the pitch slowly changed to a heavy "splash" as the pails filled.

It did not take us long to fill our pails. After pouring the milk into our jugs, we rinsed the pails, put them back on the shelf, released the cows from their gate, and finished by filling the water trough. We walked around to the front door and knocked. Tante Palma opened it and handed me a small bag. To my surprise there were several pieces of butterscotch inside. She knew this was my favorite candy.

Tante Palma said, "You can each have one now for the walk back, but save some to share with the rest of the family when you get home."

Thoralf and I thanked Tante Palma for the candy and looked at each other with wide eyes and big smiles. We each put one in our mouths, picked up our milk jugs, and started home. The walk seemed to go quickly, and soon the butterscotch taste in my mouth was only a memory. As I was thinking about having another piece, Thoralf looked up and turned his head.

"Do you hear that?" he asked.

I stopped to listen and could hear a deep, low-pitched drone. It was slowly getting louder until it drowned out all other sounds. Thoralf pointed up, screaming, "Look at that!"

Suddenly the sky was filled with hundreds and hundreds of airplanes! Big ones, small ones, all flying in formation, and all with Nazi swastikas on them. We had known about the war in Europe, but Norway had declared itself neutral. From the hill near the house, we would occasionally see warplanes in the distance over the North Sea, but never over us. Thoralf and I ran, doing our best not to spill the milk.

As we approached the house, Thelma and her friend Signy were outside pointing up at the airplanes. Mom and Bestemor were outside standing on the stairs, and I could see that all the neighbors were outside, too. Everyone was looking up and pointing at the sky. Time seemed to stop as the planes flew over, and we all stood motionless in disbelief. This lasted for several minutes, and then all of a sudden, what was happening began to sink in.

Signy's father called for her to come inside, and Mom did the same for us. As I walked in the front door, Tante Agny was in a full panic. She had already packed her bag and was headed toward the door.

"I've got to go! I've got to go!" she said. "I need to get home, if there is still a home when I get there."

We later learned that the planes had not dropped any bombs or paratroopers in our area. Mom said they were not worried about small towns like ours right now, but she was sure they would be coming in a few days if things did not go well for the Norwegian military.

April 12, 1940

Days later, Vanse was overrun by Nazis. I remember the day they came to our house. It was cool and cloudy, around noon. Mom and Bestemor were outside hanging laundry with Thelma at their side, Odd was inside emptying the washtub, and Thoralf and I were planting potatoes when a truck pulled up between our house and the neighbor's. Four German soldiers jumped out of the back. Two moved toward the Mikalsen's house, and two walked toward ours. Thoralf and I stopped our planting and walked over to the front of the house. As we did, a German officer climbed out of the passenger seat, closed the door, put one foot up on the running board, and lit a cigarette. The driver joined him, and they began talking to each other, pointing at us. I did not understand German, but their tone was calm. All of the soldiers had their rifles shouldered, and the two walking toward our house trampled the herb garden with no regard for where we had recently planted.

Bestemor stopped hanging the laundry, grabbed a nearby broom, and went running toward them.

"What are you doing?" she yelled. "Can't you see your big feet are stomping on my herbs and onions? Get out of the garden!"

Thoralf and I ran toward her, blocking her path before she reached them. The soldiers stopped in their tracks. I think they were caught by surprise. When Bestemor was mad at Thoralf and me, she chased us with the broom and we ran, but these gun-carrying soldiers were not sure what to make of an old lady shaking a broom at them. One soldier said something to the other in German, which made him laugh. Then he turned to us and in Norwegian said, "My friend likes the old lady's spunk."

He explained that they had come to Norway to protect us from the British. He said that the British were planning to mine the coastline and shipping channels to prevent cargo ships in the Baltic Sea from reaching the North Sea and Atlantic Ocean. He added that, if they did that, it would put an end to Norwegian commerce and fishing.

The soldiers pushed their way past us and walked up the steps and through the front door as if they owned the place. The one who spoke Norwegian asked Bestemor if we had any radios or guns of any kind. With a stern look, she replied that we did not have any weapons and that the house did not have electricity, so she had no use for a radio. He then asked where the man of the house was. Bestemor replied that he had died.

"The only men here are the boys who stopped me from hitting you with my broom."

He shook his head and went inside, mumbling, "Crazy old lady."

Louder he said, "Everyone stay outside while we search the house."

Mom put her hand on Bestemor's shoulder to calm her down.

The front door was left open, and we all stood on the stairs looking in. I could see only the foyer and part of the kitchen, but I could hear drawers being opened and furniture being moved. It sounded as though they were making a mess. One soldier went upstairs to search, and I could see the other in the kitchen by the table. He walked to the front door, looking at Thoralf and me, and asked, "Which of you two boys is the oldest?"

Mom quickly grabbed both of us and asked, "Why do you need to know?"

The soldier grabbed Thoralf by the shoulder and dragged him inside.

"Boy, where does this trap door in the kitchen lead?" he demanded.

"To the root cellar."

"What is down there?" he pressed.

"Potatoes, carrots, onions, peat cakes. You know, stuff we need."

"Is this the only way down?"

Thoralf shook his head. "No, there is a door on the outside. We only use the trap door during winter or heavy rains."

"Show me. Now!"

Thoralf led him out the front door, down the stairs, and to the door underneath. I could hear the door open and them walk in, but nothing after that. A few minutes later, the soldier from upstairs came down and stopped in the foyer.

"Fritz?" he called out. "Fritz, wo bist du?"

I heard the answer coming from the cellar and now knew the name of the soldier who spoke Norwegian. The soldier in the foyer came outside, pushing his way past us and calling for Fritz again. Fritz replied, and the soldier went under the stairs and into the cellar. I could hear more things being thrown around. This went on for several minutes, and when it stopped, Thoralf emerged from the cellar followed by the soldiers. The one whose name I didn't know continued back through the garden toward the truck, and Fritz walked around the house with Thoralf in tow. I heard Thoralf say that the hen house was just around the corner. A few minutes later, Fritz and Thoralf came from behind the house. Fritz had his helmet in his hand, and as he stopped in front of us, I could see that it held several eggs. Thoralf came and stood on the stairs with the rest of us.

"We did not find anything," Fritz announced. "Make sure that when we come by for regular inspections, we never find anything and you will have no problems with us. Tomorrow, you all need to go into town and have identification papers made. If you do not and are caught without them, you will be arrested."

Fritz turned and held up his helmet as he walked down the hill saying something in German. I am sure it was about the eggs. The German officer at the truck slowly put out his cigarette with his foot on the truck's running board and took the helmet from Fritz. The soldiers climbed into the truck and headed back down the hill.

When we were back inside the house, I saw the mess they had made in every room. They had opened up drawers and dumped out the contents, thrown the pillows and couch cushions on the floor, and moved all the furniture. Upstairs they had tossed everything in the storage rooms into one big pile. In the bedroom they did the same thing. All the mattresses were in a pile with the blankets and sheets at the bottom.

Mom turned to Bestemor with a worried look.

"All I have for Trygve and Thoralf are their American baptismal certificates."

"Give them to me and I will get you new ones," Bestemor replied.

Mom walked into the kitchen, and a moment later I heard her say, "Ouch!"

When she came back out, she had a wet rag placed over her forearm as she handed Bestemor two pieces of paper. Bestemor left the house. I am not sure where Mom kept the papers that the Germans did not find during the search, but I was glad they didn't. Mom told us that Bestemor would be back soon, and we should all get the house back in order before her return.

Two hours later, Bestemor walked through the door and handed Mom an envelope. She then approached Thoralf and me and said sternly, "If anyone asks you where you were born, you tell them you were both born here, in this house. Never tell anyone you were born in America."

We both reassured Bestemor we would not. Neither of us could really remember America and had never told anyone that we were born there. It only came up when Tante Agny would show pictures of us with her in Brooklyn. Bestemor nodded and then turned and walked into the kitchen.

April 14, 1940

When I arrived at Mr. Ellenes's store a few days later, I could hear the deep pitch of Mr. Dungvold's voice coming from inside. I knew that voice well from school. As I opened the front door, the bell rang, and the smell of pipe tobacco was heavy in the air. I was greeted by blank stares from several men, followed by an eerie silence.

"Ole," Mr. Ellenes said, addressing one of the men, "you were supposed to be watching for people." His voice was agitated, and he rubbed his forehead. "Trygve, Mr. Dungvold was telling us about the battle of Oslo. I need you to sweep the front porch, and if anyone is approaching—and I mean anyone, German or Norwegian—come in and tell us immediately. Try to do a better job than Mr. Amdal."

"Yes, Mr. Ellenes," I replied.

Mr. Jakobsen walked from the corner of the store and handed me the broom. He smiled and lit his pipe as he turned to walk back to the corner. I thanked him and went out to sweep. As I closed the front door behind me, I listened to Mr. Dungvold and looked for anyone who might be approaching.

"Okay, where was I? Oh yes," he started, "the German ships were coming up the Oslofjord led by their heavy cruiser, Blucher, hoping to catch the city by surprise. The 600-plus-foot cruiser had its eight-inch guns still pointing forward and aft with the muzzle covers on to look like they were coming in with no ill will, but the gun commanders protecting the city knew what they were really up to. A German ship of that size leading several support ships only meant one thing—the war was now at our doorstep."

He continued. "The Oscarsborg Fortress is a training facility at the entrance to Drobak Sound in the northern part of the Oslofjord, just south of the city, but it was short-staffed and not able to operate all the guns at full capacity. The commander woke what men there were to help load the main guns, including the cooks and maintenance people who had no gun training. They were quick learners and eager to help. They managed to get the guns loaded and ready to fire the first salvo as the German convoy approached the fortress. The gun commander waited patiently to fire until the heavy cruiser Blucher was fully abreast of the gun positions—this would give them the best chance of hitting it and doing the most damage with their first shot. This was important because he did not know if there would be time to reload and fire again with an inexperienced gun crew.

"The guns along the fort's southern placement fired first, scoring hits on the ship's bridge and on one of the main turrets. Then the eastern guns opened fire. The

Germans quickly retaliated with their smaller guns, but it took them some time to get the main guns turned and ready to fire because they had kept them in a neutral position during their approach. The forward guns had now passed the fort's gun emplacements and could not turn far enough to shoot behind them. This left the Blucher with only the aft guns to bear on the fortress. The fighting was furious. Large chunks of the fort were blown off, but the fort commander still had the aging land-based torpedo battery at his disposal. The estimated range of the ship was off, and the first torpedo hit near the bow of the ship, doing little damage. The commander made a quick adjustment and launched a second torpedo. With the adjustment, this one hit the Blucher directly, putting a large hole in its side. It was already ablaze from the gun hits and was now drifting to stop against the far shore. The commander loaded another torpedo into the tube, saving it should more of the German ships dare to pass.

"Seeing what had happened to their flagship, the remaining German ships turned and retreated to just out of range of the fort's guns to wait for the Luftwaffe's planes to come take out the fortress. The Blucher was now listing a good thirty degrees. Then there was a large explosion on board. It was their ammunition magazine. The fire must have gotten to it. This was the nail in the coffin for the Blucher. The massive ship slowly rolled over. A few minutes later, completely upside down, it began to sink, bow first. Most of the German sailors who had abandoned ship by jumping into the cold water were consumed by burning fuel as it spread around them. German paratroopers were seen by the fortress commander to be landing just outside the city. They would be getting little support from the navy, and this would surely slow their advance on the city. I am sure their first target was to capture King Haakon VII and take over the government. The brave Norwegian soldiers held off the Germans for days before they were forced to retreat north with the king and his family. I hear the Germans are still chasing after him. They will never catch him. He is much smarter than they are and will hide out or leave the country rather than be caught."

Mr. Dungvold liked telling a good story and often made them more colorful than the actual events. But, from what I could hear, it sounded as if he were actually there as it happened and had managed to escape so he could come back and tell us about it.

The talking had now fallen to a murmur, and some of the men were leaving one at a time. When Mr. Jakobsen came outside, he reached into his pocket, handed me a piece of butterscotch, and said, "The Germans don't really want us to know what is happening, and they control the newspapers. So it is good that Mr. Dungvold is able to share with us what he hears. Make sure that, if you share what you have heard today, it is with those you can really trust. Never say where or who you heard it from."

I thanked Mr. Jakobsen for the butterscotch and promised I wouldn't tell anyone. He looked at me and nodded his head. He turned and went down the few stairs and headed toward his home. Mr. Ellenes came to the door and asked me to come inside.

"Now Trygve, I need you not to speak of this to anyone. We need to know what is going on, and Mr. Dungvold says he will continue to pass along what he hears. It's for everyone's safety that we keep all information like this a secret."

I told him that Mr. Jakobsen had said for me to share what I heard only with those I could trust.

"That is good advice, but maybe you should not tell anyone, at least for now. Let's see how things turn out in the next few months. I will let you know what you can share and whom you can share it with, but, for now, better safe than sorry. There is not much for you to do here today, so you can head on home now." He handed me a bag. "Here, take this loaf of bread to your neighbors on your way. Mr. Mikalsen came in earlier today, and I told him you would bring it to him on your way home." He pushed me out the door. "The second loaf is for you and your family."

I thanked him and left to make the delivery. As I was walking home, I realized that I had seen only five men leave the store, but I was sure there had been more than that when I first went inside. What I didn't know at the time, and what I know now, is that my instinct was correct—there had been more people. Onkel Tarald was one of them.

When I left, he walked out from the back room and asked Mr. Ellenes if I had seen him.

"No, I am fairly sure he did not know you were here," Mr. Ellenes replied.

"You know we can trust him and my other nephew, Thoralf," Onkel Tarald said.

Mr. Ellenes was quick to answer.

"I am sure we can, but we cannot let either of them know about the other should we decide to let them help us in the future."

Onkel Tarald nodded and shook Mr. Ellenes's hand. "Yes, let's not involve them unless they figure things out or start asking questions. Here, let me go. We can talk more next week."

June 3, 1940

With school out for the summer and the fact that we would not be going to America any time soon, I started looking for a second job. Thoralf had managed to find full-time work at the furniture factory, but I had not been so lucky. Mr. Ellenes said that his friend, Mr. Olsen, owned the nursery on the edge of town and was looking for some help two days a week. Mr. Ellenes knew that I kept the flowers at Bestefar's grave looking nice and thought a job at the nursery might be something I would like.

As I made my way to the nursery, I noticed a group of people standing near the shore looking out toward the sea. There were three ships that looked to be anchored just offshore. My curiosity made me walk past the nursery and continue on to find out what was happening. As I got closer, I saw that two of the ships looked to be cargo ships and the third had big guns— maybe a destroyer. There were two landing crafts on the shore filled with lumber and other building materials, but the Germans were just standing on the shore and not unloading anything. Then I heard oars splashing in the water. At first I could not see where the noise was coming from, but then I saw a large rowboat full of men emerge from behind the landing craft and head toward the shore. When the rowboat ran aground, several of the German soldiers rushed over to it while yelling at the men to get out. As they did, I could see four more rowboats, all filled with men, approaching the sandy shoreline. More German soldiers broke away from the group to speed up the process. As the men exited the boats, the soldiers continued to yell and push them toward the landing craft. The Germans were making them unload the material.

I felt a tap on my shoulder. I jumped and turned around to see Mr. Jakobsen standing next to me. I asked him if he knew what was going on, and he told me that the Germans had brought Polish prisoners in to build things.

"What are they going to build?" I asked.

"Well, I would say that first they will have to build a prison camp so they have a place to sleep, and after that I am not sure, but with all these prisoners you can bet they have a lot planned," he replied.

All the prisoners were walking in a line up the hill, some pushing carts and others carrying lumber. I had never seen so many people at one time, not even when we had our Constitution Day parade. There were German soldiers guarding them, spread out alongside the long line of prisoners, but the Germans carried only their guns and backpacks. As I turned to ask Mr. Jakobsen another question, a German soldier came up to us all and told us to move along and not to talk to the prisoners.

As I turned to walk toward the nursery, Mr. Jakobsen asked me what I was doing in town, and I told him I was going to see Mr. Olsen at the nursery about a job. I explained that I had heard he needed some help, and I wanted to save up some money to buy my family gifts for Christmas this year. He said that was a nice idea and then pointed to a man walking up the hill.

"There he is. That is Mr. Olsen, the man in the hat with the cane."

I thanked Mr. Jakobsen and turned and chased after Mr. Olsen while wondering what the Germans were going to build. As I approached him, I could see he was walking with a limp, but at a brisk pace. I called out, "Mr. Olsen. Mr. Olsen."

He stopped and turned around to see who was calling his name. His face was very wrinkled. He stood tall with only a slight hunch to his back and looked to be one hundred years old, with all the gray hair coming from under his hat. I walked up to him, put my hand out, and said, "Hello, Mr. Olsen. My name is Trygve. Mr. Ellenes told me you were looking for some help in your nursery."

Mr. Olsen stood there looking at me and said nothing. His head tilted to one side and then back as if he was thinking. There were a few seconds of me awkwardly holding out my hand, and then he said, "You must be Trygve. Christian told me you would be coming to see me today." He extended his hand and shook mine. "I need someone Saturdays and Wednesdays for the next few weeks. Is that something you have time for?"

I excitingly replied, "Yes."

He looked at me, squinting his eyes a little while turning his head to one side and cupping his hand to his ear.

"YES!" I replied again, this time loudly.

"Good, good. Be at the nursery at 9 a.m., and I will show you what I need you to do. Be on time," he added as he turned and walked away.

As I headed back home, I noticed that there were now two rows of prisoners walking on the road. One row was walking up the hill carrying building material, and the other walked down the hill back toward the shore empty-handed. They were stacking the material in a clearing not far from the church. Some of the prisoners were digging holes and putting posts in the ground, while others were attaching barbed wire to them. This must be the prison camp Mr. Jakobsen was talking about.

When I reached the fork in the road, I decided to take the path up to see Mr. Ellenes and tell him what was going on. As I got closer to the store, it started to rain. I could see Mr. Ellenes on the front porch walking back into the store. It began raining harder, so I ran the rest of the way. Once under the roof of the porch, I stomped my feet, shook some of the raindrops from myself, and walked through the front door. I did not see Mr. Ellenes, but I turned and noticed that his tool section was completely bare. Mr. Ellenes, hearing the bell ring, walked out from the back room.

"Where did all your tools go?" I asked.

"The Germans came in and bought them all. Well, that's the way they see it, but I don't. They paid me in Reichsmarks. I am not sure what I can buy with that," he answered in a disgusted voice. "Wait right there."

He turned and went into the back room. He was gone for a minute or two and then came out, reached over the counter, and handed me the coping saw Thoralf had been looking at and the spare blades for it.

"Here, take this. I would rather you and your brother have it than the Germans. Tell your family they may want to hide the important things they have before the Germans stop paying for things and just start taking them."

I thanked Mr. Ellenes and told him I would pay him for the saw, but he insisted that it was a gift. I explained to him that it was too nice and that my mom would not want me to take it without paying for it. He thought for a second and said that he would pay me a little less each day I worked for him until it was paid for. I thanked him and said that would be great.

As I turned to leave, I noticed the rain had stopped. I said goodbye, thanked Mr. Ellenes again, and headed home. I knew Thoralf would be very surprised when he saw what I had.

July 19, 1940

Every morning when I walked to work, I passed the Germans marching prisoners up the hill to Kleivlands Lake. The prisoners were building a dam and running pipes down the hill to what would become an airport. When the prison camp was finished, the Germans brought in at least another two hundred prisoners to prepare the field for the airport runway. They made very good progress; the field was quickly cleared and leveled out. They also dug a ditch along one side of the runway for drainage and had built a few buildings, but I was not sure what was in them.

The prisoners' clothing was starting to look a little worn and, although they looked healthy, they were not as stout as they were when they first arrived. I did not speak or say anything to them and gave them a wide berth as we passed each other, even walking off the road to stand and let them go by.

March 7, 1941

Since I started working at the nursery, Mr. Olsen had taught me a lot about different types of flowering plants and how to use compost. Before this, I never knew there was so much to learn about manure. Mr. Olsen said horse manure was the best of them all and I had to keep all animal manures separated until the composting process was complete. When it was, he would blend the different composts depending on what we were using it for. The flowers on Bestefar's grave had never looked so good, and it was because of what I had learned from Mr. Olsen.

Mr. Olsen always saved seeds from his plants, and when we potted new crops in the greenhouse, he mixed the compost and soil and explained what type of plants to use it for. Today I was to work with Tore. He was three years older than I was and had worked for Mr. Olsen part-time since he was ten and full-time since he graduated from the eighth grade. He was an only child, and it had been just him and his mom since his father passed away when he was young. He never talked about his father, so I didn't ask. His mother, on the other hand, sounded a lot like my mom—hardworking and stern when she needed to be, but also aware that she could not do everything by herself and had to rely on her son to help as much as possible.

Tore and I would fill the small pots, put the seeds in, water them, and make sure they were properly labeled. On this day when we finished, there were two extra pots.

"Tore, what should we do with these pots?" I asked. "We have used up all the seeds Mr. Olsen gave us."

Tore thought for a second and then pulled an envelope from his back pocket.

"Let's plant these," he said.

He handed me the envelope, and inside were six tomato seeds.

"Is this all you have?" I asked.

"No, I have more to plant in my garden, but "Tomato-Fritz" comes by and takes most of them. If I had a few planted out of sight here at the nursery, then I could take some home now and again to eat right away. This way my mom and I will actually get to eat some while Fritz will still get his."

This is when I realized that everyone had a "Fritz"— we had Egg-Fritz, Tore had Tomato-Fritz, and our neighbors had Potato-Fritz. The Germans were taking something from everyone. I was just glad they had not gone as far as to live in our house.

When the Germans first arrived, they just moved in with families, and it was then the families' job to feed them. Homes near town that had electricity were the soldiers' first choice. The officers took entire buildings in town for themselves and most recently took the schoolhouse for their use.

We planted the seeds and labeled the pots as pansies. Tore placed them in the middle of all the other pots of pansies, knowing that once they sprouted we would be able to see what they really were. With that job finished, we headed outside for our next project.

September 18, 1941

On Tax Day, Bestemor got money out of a jar she kept hidden in the storeroom and gave it to Thoralf so he could go into town and pay the taxes. She told him to be careful and to go straight into town, pay the taxes, and come right back. As he went outside to get the bike, I asked Mom if I could take one of the potted pansies I was growing in the window and put them on Bestefar's grave. She said yes, so I went into the parlor and picked the best-looking one of the three. Outside, Thoralf was waiting for me. I put the plant in the bike basket, sat on the seat, and held on to Thoralf as he pushed off and began to pedal.

It was a rough ride down the hill with Thoralf standing on the pedals and me with my legs splayed out to each side with nowhere else to put them. I held on to him tighter as the ride became bumpier. We managed to make it to the bottom of the hill in one piece and coasted to the sidewalk in front of the church. Once we stopped, I grabbed the pansies and headed to the grave as Thoralf headed into town.

As I approached Bestefar's grave, I turned to see that Thoralf had stopped and was looking at the bike. He fiddled with the chain for a couple of seconds before jumping back on and heading into town. I turned back to my task and noticed that the begonias on the grave had withered from a recent frost. The pansies would make a good replacement until the heavy snows came. I knelt on the cool ground and pulled the begonia plant out, replacing it with the pansies. I told Bestefar that the Germans had come and things were not great, but Mom said not to complain and that we had to deal with what's in front of us the best we could. I patted the dirt around the freshly planted flowers and walked to the lake behind the church to get some water for them.

Maybe Mom was right. Things were not horrible, but they were keeping us from joining our father in America and, because America was not one of the countries in the war, this did not make sense to me.

When I finished watering, I walked to town to meet up with Thoralf. There was a nice watch in the general store's front window that I had my eye on, and whenever I was in town. I stopped to look at it.

When I turned the corner and started to head down the main street, I saw Thoralf about 100 yards away, coming out of the tax office. As he did, a German S.S. Officer in his black uniform and shiny black boots came out of the store next door. He was not paying attention and tripped over the bike Thoralf had laid on the sidewalk. I could not hear the conversation, but I could see the German officer pull his sidearm from its holster. He waved it back and forth, pointing it at Thoralf. I stopped dead in my tracks not knowing what was going to happen next. Thoralf bent down, and it looked as though he was rubbing the officer's boots with his sleeve. The officer put his sidearm back in the holster, and Thoralf picked up the bike and headed out of town. Shocked at what I had just seen, I turned and ducked back around the corner, out of sight. As Thoralf turned the corner, he saw me and hopped off the bike. We walked back toward the house side by side.

"Stupid Nazi," he said. "If he were paying attention, he never would have tripped over my bike."

"Why did he pull his gun out? Was he going to shoot you?"

Thoralf shook his head. "No, he was just trying to scare me."

"What did he say to you? All I could see was him motioning with his gun."

"'Du dummer Knabe, du solltest die Dinge nicht auf dem Seitenweg lassen. Wegen dir habe ich meinen Stiefel abgewetzt.'"

Even though German was part of our studies in school since the occupation, Thoralf's was a lot better than mine.

"He called you stupid?"

"He said, 'You stupid boy, you should not leave things on the sidewalk. Because of you I scuffed my boot.'"

Seeing this happen to my brother changed how I saw the occupation. Until now, I had heard stories of how the Nazis treated people, but now, seeing it firsthand, I knew them to be true. I wanted them gone from our country.

Thoralf stopped suddenly. "We cannot tell Mom about this, or she will not let us go into town anymore," he said.

"I am not going to tell her, but we need to get rid of these Nazis."

He started walking again. "There is not a lot we can do at this point. We are not soldiers."

"Well, maybe not," I said, "but there has to be something we can do."

Thoralf and I continued talking the entire walk home but could not figure out what we could do to help. For the next several days, this was all I could think about.

October 2, 1941

A couple of weeks later, I was busy cleaning the bins and shelves at Mr. Ellenes's store when he said, "I heard that your brother had a run-in with a Nazi officer in town the other day."

Caught off guard by his statement, I stopped cleaning, but only for a second. "I am not sure what you are talking about," I replied, turning to the next row.

"I can tell by the way you are acting that it is true. You need to work on your facial expressions and learn to hide your emotions in case you are ever questioned by the Nazis." he paused. "I know this occurred because Mr. Jakobsen told me he saw it happen and that he also saw you down the street."

"Yes," I admitted, "it did happen, but please do not tell my mother or anyone who might tell her."

As I thought back to what I saw, my nervousness turned to anger. "We need to get rid of these Nazis!" I yelled.

Mr. Ellenes shushed me and reminded me not to say anything out loud unless I was sure who was around. In a softer voice, he told me that, for years, all the shop owners in town had met together each month to discuss current events, but since the Nazis arrived, they were unable to have their meetings. He asked if I would like to help.

"Yes!" I said excitedly. "What do you need me to do?"

He swore me to secrecy and said I couldn't tell anyone about this, not even Thoralf.

Mr. Ellenes went on to tell me that he would schedule the meetings for after school on one of the days I would be working. He said that all I had to do was stay outside. He would have me sweep the porch, fix some of the loose nails on the front porch or, if the weather was nice, repaint the building. I was not sure how this was going to help, but then he explained my main job.

"I need you to pay more attention to the roads than on doing your assigned tasks. You need to be looking for anyone who is coming this way. If they are German, you need to knock or tap on the walls or floor three times, then once. After you knock, listen for the bell on the door. I will ring it. If you don't hear the bell, you are to come inside and find me. If they are Norwegian, you are to knock five times and then listen for the bell." he spoke deliberately. "You are to do all of this without anyone suspecting that you are doing anything other than sweeping, nailing, or painting. I will walk outside if I cannot see who is approaching from one of the windows and pretend to scold you for goofing off."

He paused to make sure I understood what he was saying. "You talk to no one about this, not even to the people you may see at the meetings. I have gotten their consent to have you help us and have assured them you can be trusted."

I told Mr. Ellenes that he could trust me and that I would do a good job for him and tell no one about it. His face softened as he put a hand on my shoulder and said, "I know you will."

On the walk home after work, I had to hide a big smile. I knew that these meetings involved more than just talking about current events, and I was very honored to be asked to help.

February 7, 1942

It had been one of the snowiest winters I could remember. It snowed almost every day from just before Christmas until now. On this day it was sunny and cold with an occasional light breeze. Peering out the front window, I saw that everything was white and glistening.

The rough terrain had been mellowed out by the snow. Just a foot or two covered the hills, whereas snowdrifts had almost filled the valleys, making the landscape resemble the swells on the sea more than its usual juts and crags. Thoralf, Odd, and I had to shovel the paths to the well, outhouse, and chickens each day, sometimes twice, because of all the snowfall.

I joined everyone else at the kitchen table to help peel potatoes while Mom was in the cellar preparing to make lefse. The potatoes were very small, ranging from three-quarters of an inch to an inch and a half. These were the potatoes that most farmers did not bother to pick from their fields. With some foods becoming harder to obtain, Bestemor thought this would be the last year the other farmers would let us go through their fields to pick what was left behind after harvest.

After peeling all the potatoes Mom needed, Thoralf, Odd, and I headed outside. Thoralf went to draw water from the well, Odd started shoveling the snow, and I went to the hen house to retrieve some eggs. When Thoralf and I returned and gave the water and eggs to Bestemor, she thanked us and told us to go outside to help Odd with the shoveling.

The path at the back of the house toward the henhouse was more like a tunnel. Six feet of snow flanked each side, and we were running out of space to put more snow. When Thoralf and I went outside, we could not find Odd, and his shovel was leaning up against the snow. Thoralf called for him, and a moment later he came around the corner.

"Where were you?' Thoralf asked.

"Carrying the snow around the corner," he replied.

"What do you mean carrying the snow?" Thoralf said bewildered. "Your shovel is right here."

"Well, I started to shovel, but there was no place to put the snow on either side of the path, so I decided to make room for it. When I put my shovel into the packed snow against the house, it fell off in a big block. I then cut the block into pieces that I could carry and put them in the garden at the end of the house. The snow is not very deep in the garden, and it is easy to walk there," Odd explained.

Thoralf and I walked to the end of the house and there they were: three rectangular blocks of snow. Thoralf and I looked at each other and almost at the same time cried, "Igloo!"

"Igloo? What's an igloo?" Odd asked.

"It's a house made of snow. Many nomadic people in Alaska and Canada make them for temporary shelters in the winter when they go hunting," I explained.

Thoralf took the shovel and started cutting more blocks from the snow against the house while Odd and I placed them in a circle, leaving a space for an entrance.

We were on our third layer of blocks, with the dome shape of the igloo now obvious, when the back door opened and Bestemor stuck her head outside. We froze in our tracks. Odd and I each had a block of snow in our hands, while Thoralf had the shovel cut into the snow.

"What are you all doing?" Bestemor asked.

We were silent for a few seconds, and then Odd spoke up. "We are building an igloo!"

Bestemor smiled, shook her head, and went back inside.

When the door closed, we went back to work. The igloo needed only a few more strategically placed blocks to close off the top. Thoralf had the hatchet and sculpted the blocks to fit before handing them to Odd and me to put in place.

The three of us stood in front of our igloo admiring our finished project.

"Are we going in it?" Odd asked.

"Sure, you go first," I replied.

"No, you set most of the blocks," Odd said with little worry in his voice. "You should get to go in first."

"Thoralf cut all the blocks, and he is the oldest, so he should get to go in first," I said as I turned toward Thoralf.

At that moment Thelma came around the corner with some snacks for all of us.

"Here, Mom told me to bring this out for the three of you for all the hard work you've been doing."

She handed us each a warm piece of fresh lefse with butter and cinnamon sugar on it, turned, bent over just a little, and walked into the igloo.

"Wow! This is neat! It's a lot bigger inside here than I thought it would be. Are you all going to come in and join me? There is enough room for all of us."

The three of us pushed each other out of the way trying to be the first—well, now the second one—in the igloo. Once inside, we sat eating our lefse and listening to Odd say one funny thing after another. Thelma was laughing more than eating. We were having fun until we heard the anti-aircraft guns followed by the sound of bombing.

The Allies must be bombing the airport again, I thought to myself.

Thelma's eyes were now wide open as she went running out of the igloo. Thoralf and I followed her.

"Where is everyone going? Is it something I said?" Odd said as he left the igloo. "Hey, wait up! I don't want to be in here by myself."

For Thelma, the igloo was a different world, a world without war. I had not seen her so happy since the war started. I was glad to be a part of her joy that day, even if it was short-lived.

April 30, 1942

The meeting of shop owners today was solemn. While outside performing my duties as gatekeeper, I could barely hear Mr. Dungvold, even with that deep voice of his. Today's news was not good, and he was speaking in what would be a normal tone for everyone else.

"It is terrible, I tell you. The Nazis are brutal. They have wiped the town of Telavåg off the map. All the buildings have been burned to the ground, and the people have been sent to concentration camps or prison camps. Lauritz Telle and his son Lars, two noble Norwegians wanting to help their country, had been secretly making runs to the Shetland Islands helping political prisoners escape and giving British Special Operations officers information they received from the XU, the Norwegian Unknown Underground. The British in turn were helping the Norwegian resistance, known as the MILORG. Somehow, the Gestapo found out and set up Lauritz and his son, but they would not go down without a fight. When the Gestapo entered the house and went upstairs, they found more than they expected.

"Sleeping in the loft were two commandos trained by the British waiting for their assignments in Norway. A gun battle ensued, and one of the commandos was killed, but not before two of the Gestapo officers were also killed, forcing the rest of them to retreat. The surviving commando chased after the Gestapo, but he had several gunshot wounds and could not keep up and soon lost sight of them. When the Gestapo returned, they did so with a vengeance. They took Lauritz, his wife, and youngest son, Åge, to Bergen to torture for information and sent Lars to a concentration camp, but their rage did not stop there. Because two Gestapo officers had been killed, all the residents were gathered up and made to watch the town as it was set on fire and burned to the ground. All the men ages 16 to 60 were sent to a concentration camp in Germany, and everyone else, including the women and children, were sent to a prison camp south of Bergen."

When Mr. Dungvold finished his story, there was dead silence for a minute, and then I heard Mr. Olsen say, "Men, we need to be more careful than ever. The Germans have made an example at Telavåg hoping to scare all other small towns from resisting. We need to be tight-lipped so this does not happen here."

I heard "yes" echo inside. The men exited one at a time over the next several minutes, each coming out with a loaf of bread or some other goods.

June 19, 1942

I woke up this morning to the sound of explosions in the distance. I quickly got dressed and stood on the front stoop to watch. The Allies had been bombing the airport the Germans built near the coast, but they were often shot down by the gun emplacements protecting it. The Germans launched their fighters very quickly, and their planes were fast. Just a week before, Thoralf and I had been sitting at the top of the hill to watch things when we heard the high-pitched whine of dive-bombers. The German Luftwaffe was out, and the dogfights were ferocious as they attacked the dive-bombers. Thoralf and I hid behind the rocks at the top of the hill while occasionally peeking over them to see the action. There were two Allied planes shot down just off the coast, while one of the German Messerschmitts had smoke trailing from it. A few seconds later, we saw a parachute. The German pilot had bailed out and was floating down to earth. His airplane was spiraling on its way down. Thoralf and I were glad to see one of the German planes shot down, and that may have been the reason we were slow to notice that the plane was no longer tracking across the sky, but was getting bigger. It was headed right for us. We both jumped up and ran to the nearby stone wall. As we jumped over it, there was a loud crash followed by an explosion. Once we were sure it was safe, we slowly stood up and saw thick black smoke coming up the hill and passing by us. We walked to the crown of the hill and saw the flames from the burning aircraft just 50 yards from where we were sitting a minute earlier. There were pieces of the burnt and mangled aircraft spread out all over of the hill.

The Allies' planes did not do much damage to the airport on this day because most of their bombs hit in the empty field just west of it. The Allies seemed to bomb the airport for a few days and then leave it alone for weeks at a time. The Germans were quick to have the prisoners repair anything that was damaged during the attacks. The current runway was made of wood, but shortly after it was completed, they started replacing the wood with stone cut from the hillside, and then they added concrete on top of that, slowly improving the runway to a more durable surface.

March 6, 1943

If it were not for Mr. Dungvold, we would not have known what was truly going on in other parts of our country. The Germans were quick to tell us about failed missions by the British and Allied forces, such as the first one against the hydroelectric dam and factory in the city of Vemork in the county of Telemark, but they never spoke of the successful missions by the Allies, such as the one Mr. Dungvold recounted on this day about the second attempt on the dam.

"This was an all-Norwegian raid!" he said. "There were six British-trained Norwegian commandos who parachuted in two weeks before the raid was to take place. They spent a few days on cross-country skis searching for the four Norwegian commandos who were still hiding out from the first attempt to destroy this target. The first attempt failed because of bad weather and because the planes with the support troops crashed. All of the men aboard were either killed from the crash or by the Germans after being interrogated. The four Norwegians who had been dropped in earlier to do reconnaissance on the target watched the two gliders crash near the landing zone. At first they went to help the British commandos, but when they arrived there were too many Germans, and the survivors had already been captured, so they returned to where they were hiding prior to the mission. But now, with more men and fresh supplies, the ten Norwegian commandos planned their attack.

"The Germans had put in mines and then added floodlights—this, along with the extra troops, meant that the ten Norwegian commandos, or the Telemark Ten, would have to be smarter than the Germans, which we all know they were. They knew a frontal assault would not work, even with a diversion, so they took an unexpected route. Their target sat atop a plateau across a ravine from their current location. They elected to repel down the ravine, cross the river below, and climb up the other side. The Germans did not expect that anyone would do this, so there were few guards on that side of the target.

"As they approached the top, they were to cross the train tracks used to move cargo in and out of the plant, but they decided to follow them into the plant instead, knowing that this route too was lightly guarded. They managed to get all the way into the plant by following the track, and as they entered, they encountered their first person. After questioning him and realizing that he was a Norwegian sympathetic to the resistance, he was asked to help. He took the lead checking to see if the coast was clear before signaling the commandos to advance. He knew that if the German soldiers saw him, he would not raise suspicions, but also knew that, being unarmed and in between the two opposing forces, he would be the first to die. He got them all the way to their target with a route that managed to avoid any contact with the Germans.

"They thanked him and started to place their explosives on the liquid-refining electrolyte chambers and water storage, while he stayed outside to alert them of any approaching soldiers. The Norwegian commandos quickly finished setting everything in place and lit the fuses. They headed back the same way they came in and managed to get outside without being detected. They had retreated into the woods before the explosions alerted the Germans to their presence. The Germans had more than 3,000 soldiers looking for them and still did not catch even one of the commandos or the Norwegian who helped them inside."

When Mr. Dungvold finished the story, I peeked through the window and could see all the men gathered around him with the exception of Mr. Jakobsen, who stood near the rear window smoking his pipe and occasionally looking outside. Some days I wished I was inside with them, but knew it was more important to be the lookout. If I ever missed any part of a story, Mr. Ellenes would fill me in after everyone left. I was not sure why they blew up water tanks; this would be my question for Mr. Ellenes.

I walked around the outside of the store one more time and didn't see anyone approaching from any direction. I went to the front door and knocked the "all clear" sign. Slowly, people left one at a time over the next 15 minutes, the last being Mr. Jakobsen. He thanked me and handed me a single butterscotch. Candy of any kind was hard to obtain now, and this was a huge treat for me. I put it in my pocket for the walk home.

With everyone gone, I went inside and asked Mr. Ellenes, "Why did they blow up water tanks?"

"Well, it is my understanding that it is some kind of special water or chemical the Germans need to build some kind of new weapon," he replied.

I shook my head and said, "If they can use water to build a bomb, what will they think of next?"

Mr. Ellenes said, "Who knows, but if we destroyed it, then maybe they will give up on it. Thank you as always. You can go home now. Here, take this loaf of bread with you."

I thanked him as I took the loaf and headed out the door to go home.

June 22, 1943

Thelma was playing in the yard while Odd, Thoralf, and I tended to the garden when we all heard gunshots. Not sure which way they were coming from, Thelma hid behind a rock, and the three of us hid behind the woodpile near the house. We had never heard so many shots all at the same time and so close to the house. The front door flew open, and Mom stepped out onto the front stoop, calling for us to come inside. As I turned to look at Mom and tell her we were safe, her head jerked suddenly, and she brushed her hair as if there were a bug in it. Then a piece of bark on the tree next to her flew off and hit the house. The shooting stopped, and Mom was still standing on the front stoop looking at the tree. She fixed her hair and told us to come inside for now. She turned and walked back into the house. We headed toward the house, and when we reached the top step, Thelma pointed at the tree. Some of the bark was missing. Thoralf looked closely and asked me for my penknife. I gave it to him, and he dug into the tree where the bark was missing.

"Look! Look what I found!" he exclaimed. "It's a bullet. It must be one from the shots we just heard!"

He handed it to me, and I realized what Mom had felt in her hair. It was not a bug. It was the bullet passing through her hair that startled her. Odd asked if he could see it.

I handed it to him and said, "This is the bullet that went through Mom's hair."

We headed inside to show her what Thelma had noticed in the tree. As we rushed into the parlor, we found Mom knitting in her usual spot.

Odd had the bullet in his hand and held it up high. "Look what we found outside in the tree by the front door. It's a bullet. Trygve said it went right through you."

"Not through her," I corrected. "Through her hair."

"Oh, through your hair. That makes more sense."

He handed the bullet to Thelma and walked into the kitchen. Mom turned to us and said, "Oh well. It must not be my time yet," and continued knitting.

Thoralf and I looked at each other and shrugged our shoulders. It did not seem to bother Mom as much as it did us. In a strange sort of way, this was calming. Thelma asked Thoralf if she could keep it, and he said yes. She then ran upstairs to put it away in her special hiding place.

September 11, 1943

Thoralf and I were walking through town, headed to the bus station with our duffel bags over our shoulders. Bestefar had called a few days earlier and left a message at Mr. Jakobsen's store asking Mom if Thoralf and I could come help him with this year's harvest. Ever since the war had started, he spent all of his time farming and none of it at sea. The number of German soldiers had been increasing each month in Norway, straining the food shortages that already existed. Farmers planted on every piece of land they possibly could because if the food ran out, it would not be the Germans who went hungry. Mom gave us permission to go, and our papers allowed us to travel back to Bestefar's town, but not much further.

As we walked down the hill, we talked about what we could remember about living there just over seven years ago.

"I wonder if Bestefar will pick us up in the rowboat," I said to Thoralf.

"No, Mom told me that the Germans improved the roads and built more bridges, so we will probably have to walk," he replied.

"I am not sure if I can remember where the house is," I said.

"You will know it when you see it. I am certain of that," Thoralf assured me as he pointed at the bus in front of the station.

As we got closer, I could see the bus, and it looked different from what I remembered. There were three cylinders connected by some piping and a fire burning to heat one of them. There also was tubing running to the front of the bus and under the hood. When we reached the back of the bus, we stopped to look at the contraption as a man from the bus company walked back to adjust something on it. I asked him what the tubing was and why it was on the back of the bus.

"This is a gasification unit," he replied. "It turns wood or coal into fuel for the bus's engine. Without it, this bus would not be able to run the route each week. The Germans give us ration coupons, but there is never any gas to give us. They use it all."

I told the man that we had the same problem with the food and other coupons we were given.

As we continued to the station, I turned to Thoralf. "Well, I hope it works because we need to get to Spangereid to help our grandparents with their farm."

When we rounded the corner, there were German soldiers at the door to the station and another two at the door of the bus checking papers.

Thoralf turned to me and said, "We will be fine, but I will go in alone to buy the tickets while you wait out here. It will draw less attention."

"Why is that?" I asked.

"Mr. Jartaag told me that the Germans don't consider kids traveling alone to be a threat until they are 16 years old, but they will question and possibly search two or more teenagers traveling together. We don't need the hassle."

I agreed, and as Thoralf went inside, I walked to the back of the bus to continue talking with the man working on the gasification tanks.

Moments later, Thoralf came out, waved for me to get in line with him, and handed me a ticket. We got our bags and helped the driver put them on top of the bus and then went to board.

As we did, the soldier at the door asked Thoralf for his papers, and he pulled them out. The guard looked them over and let him in. When it was my turn, I handed my papers to the soldier and he looked them over for a second before looking up at me and asking, "Where are you going?"

"To Spangereid," I said, looking him straight in the eye.

"Let me see your ticket."

I handed it to him. He looked the ticket over and handed it back to me.

"You know you cannot go any farther without additional travel papers, so make sure you get off the bus there. Go ahead, get on."

I told him I would and climbed on board.

"You handled that well," Thoralf said as I sat next to him, surprised.

"I don't know why he asked me and not you all those questions. Your papers and ticket say the same thing as mine."

"He knew that. He saw we had the same last name and figured you were younger and would slip up if he asked you instead of me. He must have seen us walk up together. At least he did not search our bags," Thoralf said with a hint of relief in his voice.

The bus was crammed full to Farsund, but that was also the shortest leg of the trip. We had the seat right behind the driver with a good view out the front window. When we stopped at the station in Farsund, no one got off. Outside the bus, there was a mother with two daughters who looked about our age, along with several other people waiting to get on. Thoralf got off to help the driver with the luggage, so I followed him. The mother thanked us for helping, and the three of them got on the bus. I could see that they were taking our seats.

"Good going, Thoralf. Now we will have to stand," I said as I handed him another bag.

When we had finished and went to get on the bus, it was completely full with no standing room left.

Thoralf and I looked at each other, and I just shook my head at him. The driver yelled to us from his seat, "Well, if there is any room on the roof, the two of you can ride on top until the next stop. Maybe someone will get off there, and then there will be room for you inside."

"This is all your fault, Thoralf." I muttered. "You see a pretty face, and it just causes problems."

We climbed up the ladder, wedged ourselves in between the luggage, knocked on the roof twice, and we were on our way.

It wasn't as bad a ride as I thought it would be, but I wasn't going to let Thoralf know that. We had to stay on the roof all the way to Spangereid. Each time the bus stopped, we handed down luggage and then packed the new pieces around us.

When we arrived in Spangereid, the bus rounded a corner before coming to an abrupt stop. I looked around; everything seemed different. A few people got off, including the driver. We handed down luggage to the passengers and climbed off. The bus driver thanked us for being good sports about the ride, and we thanked him for not making us wait for the next bus.

I noticed that the bus station was not the same one we had departed from years ago, and I said as much to the driver.

He looked at me oddly for a second and then said, "Oh, the station was moved here after the old one burned down three years ago."

I now wondered what else had changed during my absence.

I turned around admiring all the new buildings and was pleasantly surprised to see Bestefar walking toward us, puffing on his pipe. He was wearing overalls and a white shirt that was not so white on the sleeves. He was also wearing the same hat that I remembered from sitting on his lap while listening to his stories. We both ran and hugged him, and as I did, I inhaled the familiar scent of pipe tobacco.

"Look at the two of you! You are as tall as I am now," he said. "Bestemor will not recognize you. She thinks her little grandsons are coming to see her, and you are not so little any more. Come on, let's go. She has made your favorite dinner and just might have something special afterward for the two of you."

During the walk up to the house, Thoralf and Bestefar were already talking about work and what needed to be done first. Thoralf had made this trip last year by himself after he had graduated from the eighth grade. While they talked, all I could think about was what Bestemor might have made for us for dessert.

We walked up the front stairs, and Bestefar threw open the front door and yelled for Bestemor.

"Look what I found wandering in the street!"

I could hear someone in the kitchen and could smell and hear fish frying. I took a deep breath trying to figure out what treat Bestemor had made for us, but the smell of frying fish was overpowering, and dessert would have to remain a surprise. She came out of the kitchen with her arms wide. Thoralf and I hugged her and then stood in front of her as she looked us over.

"You are both so tall and so handsome. Thoralf, Ingrid asked me if you were coming again this year. I think she likes you. Trygve, did you bring your journal? Do you have lots of interesting stories like the ones Thoralf told me last year?"

I replied, "I do have a lot of things to tell you about, but I forgot to bring my journal."

Thoralf looked at me and then down at the floor and around the room to avoid eye contact.

What I couldn't tell her was that the journal had been taken by the Germans on one of their inspections of our house. The day it happened I had been caught off guard and did not have time to hide it as they barged in. When they opened it and saw all the handwritten notes with dates, they thought that we were spying on them. Someone handed Fritz, the soldier who spoke Norwegian, the book. He opened it up, read the first page and then a few others, and looked at me. Then he looked at the other soldiers and said, "It is just a child's writing." Without waiting for a response, he threw it into the fire. I was so mad and at the same time confused. I knew he had read that I was born in Brooklyn, New York, but he didn't say anything about it.

As I was thinking back to that incident, I must have zoned out because soon I felt a gentle shake.

"Trygve, Trygve, did you hear me?" Bestemor asked, her hand on my shoulder. "It's okay that you forgot it. You can tell me about things tonight after dinner."

I looked up at her and said, "That would be great. I have so much to tell you."

She put her arm around me and walked me into the kitchen.

"Come, Thoralf, let's all sit down and eat while it is still hot. Odin, take your seat," Bestemor said as she placed the fish on the platter next to the steamed carrots and potatoes.

Bestefar broke off a piece of bread and passed the loaf to Thoralf. Bestemor sat down and thanked the Lord for getting her two grandsons to her safely and in good health. The smell of fish filled the room, and I could tell it was cod. It smelled and tasted just as I remembered it—very tender with just a little seasoning. It did not take Thoralf and me long to finish dinner. As I took the last bite of potato, I could smell cardamom. This to me meant fyrstekake! I was smiling as I said to Bestemor, "Bestefar said you made a special treat for dessert today. Can I ask what it is?"

"Nope," she replied. "I will show you."

As she got up from the table, Bestefar said, "She has spent a lot of time trading with people to get all the ingredients and only this morning got the last one."

As she walked back to the table with a towel-covered plate, I was sure I was right. Bestemor placed it on the table in front of Bestefar and handed him a knife. His eyes were opened as wide as Thoralf's in anticipation. Since the occupation started, any treat or dessert was a rare occurrence.

Bestemor uncovered the plate and there it was— fyrstekake, the perfect dessert. The basket weave design on the top was browned just slightly, and the outer edges were browned a little more. The aroma was intoxicating and made my stomach grumble in anticipation. It was not as big as she usually made them, but there was plenty for the four of us.

As Bestefar cut it into four pieces, Bestemor said, "I could not get enough almonds, so I had to make this one smaller than usual."

In unison, Thoralf and I said, "This is plenty, thank you."

I ate it slowly, savoring each bite, and when I finished I looked around the table and noticed that Bestemor, sipping her coffee with a big smile, had not even taken her first bite. I did not have this kind of control when a dessert was placed in front of me.

I looked at her and smiled, thanking her again for a wonderful dinner and asked, "Bestemor, why haven't you eaten any of your fyrstekake?"

She put her coffee down, looked at Thoralf and me, and said, "I have missed the two of you so much that having you here with me is better than any dessert."

There was a short pause before Bestefar said, "Well, if you are not going to eat it, then it should not go to waste." he reached over to take her slice.

Bestemor grabbed the plate, moving it aside. "You are right. It should not go to waste. I will save it for after tomorrow's dinner and then cut it in two for my grandsons to share after a long day's work."

Bestefar leaned back and put his pipe in his mouth. He reached into his pocket and said, "I seem to be out of pipe tobacco. Thoralf, why don't you walk with me down the hill to the general store while Trygve stays here and tells Bestemor about some of the stories from his journal?"

Thoralf and Bestefar excused themselves and left the room. I helped Bestemor clear the table and offered to help wash the pots and dishes, but she would not have that. She pushed me away and told me to sit at the table as she washed. "Sit and tell me one of the stories in your journal," she said.

As I sat back down, I saw Thoralf coming down the stairs with a small package. He handed it to Bestefar, who put it under his hat as they went out the door. They were not gone long, and when they returned, I was telling Bestemor about the time Onkel Tarald took us fishing for my birthday.

Bestemor and I talked for hours after Bestefar and Thoralf went to bed. It wasn't until I yawned that she told me to go to bed. I would have to be up early the next day and could continue sharing my stories then.

September 12, 1943

The next morning we were up early with eggs and bread for breakfast before heading out the door. Bestefar, Thoralf, and I walked next door to Mr. Selvig's farm and we were soon joined by several of the neighboring farmers with their family members.

Harvest time was a team effort. As usual, Mr. Selvig's tractor had problems, but with no gasoline available that did not matter. The first four days were devoted to potato harvesting. We were divided into teams, with the oldest men plowing the ground or leading the horse carts while the youngest boys and the women picked the potatoes from the freshly tilled soil and placed them in baskets. The stronger and taller men dumped the baskets into burlap sacks and placed them on the carts. This was a very efficient process and nothing like what we did back home.

Thoralf and I were given small shoulder bags and told to put potatoes smaller than two inches in them— they would be used as next season's seed potatoes. With this assignment, Thoralf and I were part of the potato-picking crew and spent the entire day bent over, collecting and putting them into baskets. As soon as we started to work, Thoralf slowly fell behind me in the group of 30-plus pickers, and it became obvious why—he was right next to Ingrid talking up a storm. He was telling her about our bus trip and that we had braved the elements atop the bus to get here.

As I listened, I started to laugh. "Tell her why we ended up on top of the bus."

I turned and saw him giving me a look as he considered what to say next, but before he said anything, I continued.

"There was an elderly woman and her family who needed help with their luggage. Thoralf not only offered to help them, but also, when we finished, he gave them our seats so they would not have to stand. My brother is always thinking of others first. Like this morning, he let me sleep in and did all the morning chores Bestemor had given us to do while we are here. In fact, he told me just before we started picking potatoes that he would let me sleep in all week."

I turned around again with a smile and saw Thoralf glaring at me, as if maybe I had gone too far. At that moment Ingrid said, "Thoralf, that was so mature of you to help those people on the bus and give them your seats and then to help your little brother, too. You have matured a lot from last year when I first met you."

Now I was sure I would get to sleep in late for the next few days.

September 16, 1943

When I came down for breakfast in the morning, Bestemor asked me if I was feeling okay.

"Yes," I replied. "Why do you ask?"

She said, "I noticed that Thoralf was doing all the chores while you were still sleeping. I asked why he didn't wake you to help him, and he said that you were not feeling well and he wanted to let you sleep in."

I turned to look at Thoralf. He was grinning more than usual as he ate his oatmeal, and he tried not to make eye contact with me. I could not tell Bestemor the real reason I was sleeping in, so I replied, "I am just tired from all the long days," and sat at the table.

"Oh? Thoralf said you were probably sick, so I was ready to give you some castor oil, but if you are just tired, then you just need more food. I will fry you some eggs while you eat your oatmeal."

Now I was grinning as Thoralf sank into his seat. When the eggs came, I thanked Bestemor and asked her for another plate. When she handed one to me, I slid one of the eggs onto it and put the plate in front of my brother.

"We're even," I said.

He looked up at me, smiled, and said, "Ingrid has a friend."

September 25, 1943

Thoralf and I were heading home today, hopefully not on the roof of the bus this time. As we sat eating our breakfast—nothing special, just the usual oatmeal with bread—Bestemor was too busy to sit with us. I am sure it was because she was sad about our leaving. Bestefar thanked us over and over for coming to help. The past two weeks made it obvious to me that he was not a young man anymore and that farming was hard on him.

When we stood up from the table, Bestemor handed Thoralf a small bag with cinnamon sugar lefse in it and gave him a hug.

"You share this with Trygve," she said as she began to cry.

Then she turned, wiped her eyes, and hugged me. "You come back next year and maybe bring Odd with you."

I hugged her even harder, told her I would try, and thanked her for all the good food and conversation. It was hard to leave, but Bestefar said we needed to go or else we would miss the bus.

Thoralf and I grabbed our bags and left with Bestefar for the bus station. When we reached the bottom of the hill and turned the corner, Ingrid was standing there. She had obviously been waiting for Thoralf. I looked at Thoralf, and he had that stupid smile on his face. I took his bag, told him to meet us at the bus station, and Bestefar and I continued walking. When we finally boarded the bus after all of our goodbyes, it was not very crowded, and we had seats inside for the entire trip.

February 25, 1944

I was in the back pulling the last loaves of bread from the oven when I heard Mr. Dungvold's distinct voice. Mr. Ellenes stuck his head through the doorway and told me to hurry up and get outside because the other shop owners would be arriving soon. I took the last loaf out of the oven, took my apron off, and put on my jacket, hat, scarf, and gloves. As I walked to the front door, I said hello to Mr. Dungvold, and he handed me the broom and a shovel.

"The snow is coming down pretty hard out there," he said. "I will try to not have you out too long. Maybe I will give people fifteen minutes to get here and then start whether they are here or not. If they are late or don't come because of the snow, then they will have to wait until our next meeting to hear what I have to say."

When I first got outside, the cold felt refreshing after working by the oven, but then a gust of wind blew snow around the corner, and I hoped Mr. Dungvold would be short-winded. As I shoveled the snow off the front porch, shop owners began arriving. Mr. Jakobsen showed up first, followed by Mr. Amdal, Dr. Halversen, and then Mr. Larsen. I was surprised to see him with all the snow and wind. He had given his skis to relatives who lived in the mountains because they had broken theirs, so he had to walk, but he also had the shortest distance to travel. Everyone else had skied here. They each cleaned off their equipment and took it inside so there would not be several pairs of skis on the front porch, visible to anyone who might pass by. Even though I was sure no Germans would be coming in this bad weather, the only skis outside were mine, as it should be.

As I finished the front porch, I heard Mr. Dungvold begin. I started my walk around the outside of the store, looking to see if anyone was approaching. There would be no painting or checking for loose nails today, only walking around the building. The wind was howling, and I had to keep adjusting my scarf to keep my face as warm as possible. Even though there was a small slit between my scarf and hat so I could see, I spent most of the time squinting. With the scarf and the wind blowing, I could not hear anything from inside and would have to learn the story another day. By my third time around, I had made a nice path in the snow on one side. The wind gusts were so strong that the blowing snow filled in my tracks on the other three sides, leaving no evidence that I was ever there. I was getting colder with each lap and started to shiver by the fifth one. I stopped only for a few extra seconds on the downwind side of the building to brush off all the snow that was sticking to me in an attempt to stay dry. Mr. Dungvold seemed to be long-winded today, and I was shaking so hard that I had a hard time keeping my balance in the wind.

To my relief, I didn't have to wait much longer because I heard the knock that indicated they were finished. I was on the exact opposite side of the building from the front door and quickly turned to head toward it to give the all-clear response. It was taking me so long to get there that they knocked again waiting for my reply. As I tried to get up the few stairs at the front porch, I fell and do not remember how I got inside, but I woke up on a cot in the back room with Dr. Halversen rubbing my legs and feet. I could see my clothes hanging across the room near the bread oven. I shivered slightly and slowly sat up. Mr. Ellenes brought me a cup of coffee to help warm my insides.

"Tyrgve," he said as he handed me the cup, "if you ever have any issues during our meetings, you need to let us know. Just signal that someone is coming and then come inside and tell us. We all appreciate your dedication to the job, but not at the expense of losing you. Fortunately for us, Ole looked out the front door and saw you lying in the snow. He ran out, scooped you up, and brought you inside and then went back out to take your place."

"Is he here? I would like to thank him," I replied.

"No, he left as soon as I told him you would be okay, and so did the others," Dr. Halversen said. "Just Christian and I are here with you. You will need another 30 minutes or so before you should head home."

"I will go with him to make sure he gets there and makes it inside," Mr. Ellenes insisted.

"Good, then I will be on my way."

Dr. Halversen handed me my warm clothes to put on and added, "I guess the one good thing about this happening is you now know your limits. This could be helpful for you in the future."

Mr. Ellenes walked with him to the front door as I got dressed. My clothes, now dry and warm, felt wonderful as I put my arms and legs into them. This reminded me of what Mom would do for us on the coldest days before we left for school or work—she, too, would hang our clothes near the oven to warm them. That memory seemed as if it were from ten years earlier, but it was just the previous year. As I started to think about what it was like before the occupation, Mr. Ellenes walked back in.

"We need to leave soon if I am going to go with you and still make it back to my house before curfew. I need you to get up and walk around more. Lars told me to see how your coordination was and to make sure you will be okay. If not, I am to take you home with me."

"I will be fine," I replied. "Besides, if I go home with you, my mom will worry all night about where I am."

"That she will. Your mom and grandmother are doing a great job raising the four of you." he paused for a moment and then said, "Let's bundle up, get our skis on, and head out."

As we put everything on, he recounted what Mr. Dungvold had told them. Mr. Ellenes even waved his arms around a little as Mr. Dungvold did when he got excited.

"The Vermork factory and dam were repaired after the Telemark Ten's assault a few months ago. With all the reinforcements the Germans added, another ground-based assault would be costly, so the Allies have been bombing it repeatedly. After months of bombing, the Germans decided to ship the remaining heavy water to Germany. One of the local commandos was given this information and knew they would be using the ferry to get it across Lake Tinn. He recruited two local resistance fighters and built a time-delayed bomb. They hid it in the bottom of the ship.

"As the ferry crossed the lake and was at its deepest point, the bomb went off, blowing a large hole in the hull. The ferry filled with water and sank, taking the Germans' cargo with it to the bottom. Unfortunately, a few Norwegian passengers drowned in the lake. The resistance fighters had to make a choice; if they had warned the passengers and the ferry was empty, the Germans would have been suspicious." His voice was glum. "It is a terrible price that is paid in this war, but there is no other way sometimes. I hope this war will be over soon."

April 15, 1944

Food was getting harder, if not impossible, to buy. We often had food ration stamps for items that were limited or not available. The same went for fabric, clothing, and, most importantly, shoes. I had always gotten Thoralf's shoes when he outgrew them and then Odd got mine, but since there were no new shoes, we were each wearing ones that had gotten too tight. Mom and Bestemor reused every scrap of clothing we had. Thelma's dresses were made from some of Mom's old dresses, and the scraps left over from that were saved to be used as patches or to make clothing for Thelma's doll. Nothing got thrown away.

Because Bestemor was known as the best spinner in Lista, she was very busy on her spinning wheel these days. The ladies who came to drop off their wool would say, "Your Bestemor makes the best yarns. Whether I ask for fine, medium, or coarse, she creates the most consistent and smoothest yarns to be found anywhere."

With her services in demand more than ever, people brought items for trade. Sometimes they brought more than Bestemor would accept. She said that everyone was having hard times, and to take more than we needed was not fair. Occasionally, she would not accept anything, telling the person, "If I take more than I can use now, it will do both of us no good because when the Germans come by, they will just take it for themselves."

Almost everybody understood this mindset because they had experienced it firsthand. Thoralf and I had created several places in which to hide things. Some were in the attic below the floorboards. In the cellar, we stacked the peat cakes with hollow spots in the middle. We even left most of the potatoes in the ground to keep the Germans from taking all of them at one time. I am sure everyone else had places to hide things. We did not have many valuables, at least not the monetary kind, but we did have some things that meant a lot to Mom and Bestemor.

Against her better judgment, Mom had been letting Thoralf and me go fishing and trapping whenever we had time. By now we knew most of the Germans' routines and could easily avoid them. We occasionally went fishing at Kleivlands Lake even though Mom and the Germans made it forbidden. When the Germans dammed up the lake, it caused the stream to run dry while the lake filled. The other small lakes near us had been fished out, so if we wanted to eat, that is where we needed to go. Thoralf and I did not mention this to anyone, especially Mom.

After finishing lunch, we headed out to fish, and Mom said Odd could join us. We left through the back door in the storage room, hopped over the stone wall, and started across the field up the hill toward a small pond to the west.

As we walked, Odd broke the silence.

"How come I am carrying most of the stuff?"

"Because you were the first one out the door and grabbed it all," Thoralf responded quickly. "It's not my fault you only left the bait for me to carry."

"And I knew if I took my time, the two of you would grab everything," I added. "Here, give me the fishing poles. After we bait the snares and are done fishing, everyone carries their own catch and gear home."

"I can't carry 10 fish home by myself," Odd boasted.

I rolled my eyes. "No, Odd, I said everyone carries their own stuff home. You won't have to carry my fish."

Thoralf snorted. "The day either of you catch 10 fish, I will carry them home for you."

As we walked further, I thought about some of the conversations I had heard at the shop. Many of the men who met at Mr. Ellenes's store had talked about evasive tactics and what to do in various situations. Some of this I was about to tell Odd.

After reaching the far side of the field and climbing over another stone wall, we headed into the woods. When we got about 50 yards in, I asked Odd if he actually wanted to catch some fish today.

He gave me a confused look.

"Of course I do. What do you mean?"

Thoralf looked at me, and I continued.

"Well, as you know, the pond we are heading to is fished out, and the only water left with a lot of fish is Kleivlands Lake."

"I knew the two of you were fishing at the lake the Germans dammed up!" he replied.

"Did you tell anyone?" Thoralf asked.

"I know better than to say anything to anyone," said Odd, a little perturbed at the two of us for even thinking it. "I am not Thelma."

"Don't pick on Thelma," I told him sternly. "She is still too young to truly understand what's going on and what needs to be done. That is why Mom keeps reminding her not to say anything to any of the Germans unless asked a question, and even then to say very little."

"Okay, okay," Odd replied. "Let's catch some fish."

I explained that I had waited to ask him until we were deep enough into the woods so that, if we were being watched from afar, no one would be able to see when we changed directions.

"This is important to know if you are ever chased by someone," I said. "Changing directions at the right time is key to a good evasion, and you shouldn't head in the direction you ultimately want to end up in, if possible. The Germans are crafty and will try to cut you off."

As we approached the edge of the woods closest to the lake, we stopped and listened. Sound traveled well across the lake, and the Germans always seemed to travel in pairs and could not shut up or be quiet for more than 20 seconds unless an officer was around. Their routine varied, but they always came up to the lake by the construction road they had put in to build the dam. After hearing nothing, we moved toward the last row of trees before the clearing. Each of us was as quiet as possible as we looked in different directions. Then we looked at each other and nodded. The coast was clear.

Odd and I set and baited snares, hoping to catch a rabbit or some small game birds while we fished. Thoralf had the best eyes and ears and kept watch to make sure we were not surprised.

"Come on, hurry up," he said. "I could have had all the snares set by now."

I looked at him. "We are trying to set the snares, not set them off."

"I'm done!" Odd said in an excited but muffled voice. "I knew I would beat you, Trygve."

"You let him beat you again?" Thoralf asked.

I shrugged. "Yes, but he has never caught more fish than me."

"I tied once," Odd shot back.

"Yes, once a tie, but never more."

With the snares set, we headed across the clearing to a small group of trees near the shore. We walked with the shade of the trees behind us for as long as we could so that we would not stand out. Once we reached the edge of the lake, we sat with our backs tight against a tree, baited our lines, and casted them out. We each faced in a slightly different direction, looking and listening for anyone who might be approaching, German or Norwegian. I knew of no Norwegian traitors or Nazi sympathizers in our area, but did not want to be seen and recognized in case there was the slightest chance of even a good Norwegian succumbing to Nazi pressure or torture or, even worse, telling Mom we were up here. If we were to have any conversation while fishing, it could only be at a whisper.

A few hours passed and we had nothing to show for it. Thoralf started to whistle like a goldfinch. Odd and I looked at him and he handed us some bread to eat. A few minutes later, as we were finishing our bread, Odd got a nibble and pulled in his line with a 15-inch trout. I had never seen Odd catch the first fish without saying anything, though he did have a large smile on his face. He was very good at being quiet and it must have been killing him. Thoralf and I smirked at his silence. The fish were now biting, and over the next hour, we caught a total of 13. Since this is considered unlucky, we thought about throwing one back, but as hungry as we had been most days, that was not really an option, so we kept fishing and decided we would leave as soon as we caught one more. We sat there until the sun dipped low on the horizon and we needed to go, but we still had only 13 fish.

We were all so intent on catching another fish that we had not noticed the two German soldiers now stopped at the dam. One was getting out of the sidecar as the other remained sitting on the motorcycle, lighting a cigarette.

Odd looked at us, clearly worried, and whispered, "What are we going to do now?"

"Just sit still and be quiet," Thoralf responded. "They might not even come this way."

"Let's bring our lines in and get ready just in case," I said.

The two soldiers stood by the motorcycle, smoking and talking to each other. They were about a quarter of a mile away. Odd was getting nervous and wanted to run.

I reminded him that if we needed to run, we couldn't run in the direction of home until we were sure we were not being followed. The Germans would cut us off.

"If Thoralf tells us it is time to run," I said, my eyes still on the soldiers, "we all need to get up and go—no indecision or one of us might get caught. We'll stay together as long as we are not seen."

I looked at them before continuing. "Since there are only two of them, if they do see us, we'll need to run in different directions. That way, only two of us risk being chased and it is more likely they will stay together and chase only one of us. They are slow and out of shape, so if they do come after us, they will not last long."

"How do you know all of this?" Odd whispered.

"Thoralf and I will tell you later," I responded. "For now, just make sure you do what you are told."

The two soldiers were slowly walking along the shoreline in our direction as they continued their conversation.

"What are we waiting for?" Odd asked, panicked. "They're getting closer."

Thoralf pointed up. "Look at the direction of the shadows from the trees. See how the sun is just a little above the horizon and the Germans are almost in a line between us and the shadows? I am waiting for all of these to line up."

"That way," I continued, "if we manage to leave before the sun sets completely, they will be blinded when looking in our direction."

"How do the two of you know all of this?" Odd asked again.

We didn't answer.

"Okay," Thoralf said instead. "Get ready."

The next 20 seconds felt like an hour. The Germans had stopped at another small group of trees at the shoreline, looking off toward the lake.

"Now," Thoralf said. "Let's go."

We got up quietly with all of our gear and fish and started to head across the clearing toward the woods. We stayed tight together, walking quickly as one. We were so close to each other that Odd's foot got tangled with Thoralf's, and he fell to the ground. I tripped over him and the fish fell. Then we heard what we did not want to hear.

"Halt! Halt!" Shouted one of the soldiers.

Thoralf looked at us.

"Split up! Odd, run in the direction of the setting sun until you get to the woods, and then change direction. Make your way to the hunting blind Onkel Tarald showed us, and stay there until you are sure you are not being followed. Trygve, you know what to do."

The three of us raced off in different directions. Odd had the shortest distance to travel to get to the woods. As I turned my head to see if he had made it, I saw him with the sack of fish I had dropped. He was still 25 yards from the thick trees.

"Halt! Halt!" The guards shouted again, but this time, the command was followed by two gunshots.

As I entered the other edge of the woods, I stopped just for a moment behind a large tree to see if one of my brothers had been shot and was lying in the clearing. I was relieved to see nothing but trees, and I could hear Thoralf running through the woods, making as much noise as possible to draw the Germans away from Odd and me. He had a great sense of direction and could weave a path through the woods at night that no one else could follow. The German soldiers were still running up the hill but had not even made it to the spot where we had been fishing.

I took off down the hill and heard two more gunshots. There was no more looking back for me—it was now a full sprint down the hill. It was getting darker, and there was only the light from the half-moon shining through broken clouds. The wind was calm, and the temperature was dropping quickly. It was hard to see, so all of my concentration was on the ground where my feet landed and not so much on the branches that kept hitting my face and body. I ran with my arms up trying to protect my face as much as possible.

I stopped every few minutes or so to listen, when a good hiding place presented itself. The first time I stopped, I could still hear voices in the distance, but they were muffled and hard to make out. Unsure whether they were German, I continued in a direction away from the lake and away from Bestemor's house. The next time I stopped, I heard neither talking nor movement. Not sure if the Germans were also being still and listening, I continued for another five minutes. When I stopped for a third time, I still didn't hear anything and was sure that they were either chasing one of my brothers or had given up, if they had been chasing me.

I began to work out which direction to take to make my way back home. I hoped that Thoralf and Odd were already there waiting for me. After making my way to the edge of the woods, I followed the tree line around to the stone wall that encircled the field behind our house. As I headed across the open field, I started to wonder how much trouble we were going to be in for staying out after curfew. I walked slowly toward the house hoping that, if I were the last one home, the others would have already taken most of the blame and the brunt of the yelling that would surely come our way.

As I approached the rear of the house, I noticed that the lantern by the back door was not lit. Thoralf and I had agreed to light this lantern if the other was not home after dark and it was safe. The unlit lantern meant one of two things: either Thoralf was not home, or he was and the Germans were there. Odd might be home, but he did not know about the signal.

Once I was at the part of the stone wall closest to the back of the house, I could see through the kitchen window. Mom was pacing back and forth in front of it every few seconds. When I reached the back door, I heard her footsteps but no yelling. This meant I was the first one home. I lit the lamp by the back door and entered the house. As I did, the door hinges creaked and the footsteps stopped. I was not looking forward to what was coming my way.

Thelma later told me that Mom was very worried when Thoralf, Odd, and I had not arrived home yet. She, Thelma, and Bestemor were in the kitchen waiting for us. Thelma was peeling potatoes, and Bestemor was dicing carrots.

"Where are the boys? They know they're supposed to be home by curfew," Mom said, pacing back and forth.

"I'm sure they will be home any minute," Bestemor said. "You'll see. They will walk in as soon as I get the food on the stove."

Once everything was cut up, Bestemor put the potatoes and carrots in a pot of water to boil. Mom was still pacing back and forth, now with a handkerchief in her hand. She would use it occasionally to wipe her eyes, but mostly she rolled it in her fingers and then refolded it. This went on for almost an hour, interrupted only when she thought she had heard something. Bestemor added more water to the pot of vegetables to keep them from burning.

Bestemor and Thelma were sitting at the table playing Old Maid when they heard the back door open. They both turned to look toward the storage room, and Mom stopped in her tracks. She heard the door squeak and then the latch grab as it closed. Then the storage room door opened, and I walked in.

Mom ran over and gave me a big hug. Bestemor and Thelma soon joined us. The group hug lasted for at least 15 seconds and was very reassuring.

"Are you okay? Where are your brothers? You know you are not supposed to be out so late. Where are your brothers?" Mom said through tears, her voice stern.

Thoralf and I never told Mom the truth about things like this, but I was not sure what Odd would say, so I changed the location of what happened and made it sound a little less stressful than it truly was.

"We were all fishing at the pond and were having such a good time talking. We weren't catching any fish, so we split up and spread out around the pond. Then the fish started to really bite, and we forgot to pay attention to what was going on around us. Next thing we knew, we heard the Germans coming, so we all ran in different directions. I am sure that the Germans did not catch Thoralf or Odd. Odd was on the far side of the pond, and Thoralf was the closest to the Germans, but he quickly ran into the woods as they approached. The Germans started to chase Thoralf but stopped at the edge."

I knew when Thoralf got home he too would not tell Mom the truth. We had had many discussions about this and decided we were all better off if she did not know what we did to help feed the family. I was not sure what Odd was going to say, but I hoped that they were both okay.

As I headed to the table, Thoralf arrived in the kitchen through the storage room door. He looked at me and I at him, both of us wondering where Odd was.

The hugging and questions started again, this time with Thoralf at the center. I used this opportunity to briefly relate my story again so that Thoralf would know what I had told everyone. He was quick to confirm and fill in a few details of his own.

"The Germans did not chase me long," he said. "Halfway down the hill, I lay between two fallen trees and waited to be sure they had given up their search. When I heard the motorcycle start in the distance and drive away, I knew they were gone and took my time coming home, making sure not to cross the path of any other soldiers on the way."

Mom began crying again. "Where is your brother? Where is Odd? You know he is not as fast as the two of you and gets tired easily."

Having had polio, Odd often used this excuse when he was younger to get out of doing his chores, but from what I saw as he ran from the soldiers, he would not be getting away with that anymore, at least not with me.

I could smell potatoes burning. Bestemor went to the stove and poured more water in the pot. Normally when I could smell food cooking, it would make my stomach grumble, but that was not the case this time. My stomach felt as if it were tied in a knot. I'm sure it was from worrying if Odd was safe. Mom's relief at Thoralf's and my return was wearing off, and her anger was starting to come through. To my surprise, at that moment, Odd walked into the kitchen with the fish we had caught held up high.

"I am sorry I am late," he said, "but Trygve dropped the fish and I was hungry, so carrying all of this slowed me down. Did I miss anything?"

Mom looked stunned and then started to cry. She grabbed Odd and squeezed him harder and for longer then she had hugged Thoralf or me.

"I thought the Germans had gotten you and I would never see you again. I was so worried!"

She hugged Odd again and then turned to Thoralf and me.

"Don't you do that to me again." she looked at each of us individually. "Don't any of you do that to me again."

She grabbed the fish, went to the sink, and she and Bestemor cleaned them, fried them, and fed them to us for dinner on top of the now-mashed potatoes and carrots. Dinner was very quiet that evening, and the three of us went to bed right afterward.

September 16, 1944

The four of us were walking to pick hazelnuts from the two trees at the top of the hill. We all liked to eat them, and they stored well through the winter. Odd liked to mash his into a paste on the big stone in the basement and mix it with butter to put on his bread. He called it filbert butter. The rest of us thought this was crazy, but he liked it, and Mom didn't care as long as he cleaned the stone when he was finished.

As we approached the top of the hill, I could feel the cool breeze that was forced up the hillside from the North Sea when the winds blew from the south. It felt and smelled wonderful. It made me want to be out on the sea fishing again, but with the German occupation that was not possible.

When we reached the top, we spread an old sheet under one of the trees, and Odd and Thelma stood on the edges so that the wind wouldn't carry it away. Thoralf and I climbed up the tree and shook the branches, causing the nuts to fall onto the sheet below. We managed to shake most of them down, but there were still some left in the tree. They grew in bunches along the limbs, so Thoralf and I grabbed the remaining nuts by the handful, pulling them loose and dropping them down. Thelma and Odd placed some rocks on the sheet and started to help by grabbing the nuts they could reach from the ground.

We finished the first tree and moved onto the one closest to the water. While in it I spotted activity at the airport along the coast below. The Nazis had finished the airport two years earlier. There were airplanes stationed there, along with anti-aircraft guns, but on this day something different was happening. I saw what looked like two staff cars and a group of men standing near them. I noticed a tank pulling out a long ramp from the bunker carved into the mountain, and there was a very small plane on it. I did not see a propeller and was not sure how it would fly.

Odd yelled up at me. "What are you doing? Taking a nap?"

I climbed out of the tree and pointed toward the airport.

"Look what just came out of the bunker. It is a small plane on a ramp."

Thoralf climbed down from the tree, and we stood next to each other and stared at the airport. Then we heard a deep pulsing sound echoing through the mountains. Odd pointed as the small plane was catapulted up off the ramp and into the air. At first it dropped down slightly, but then it slowly gained altitude. Thelma ran and hid behind some rocks while the three of us stared in amazement.

Thoralf said, "I have heard of the Nazis using flying bombs."

"Yes, buzz bombs," I replied. "That must be what that is."

Thelma popped her head up for just a moment and said, "Whatever it is I don't like it. I don't like anything about this war. Because of it we are all stuck here without Pop. I hate it!"

Crying, she ran down the hill toward the house. I chased after her while Thoralf and Odd finished gathering up the nuts. I caught up with her just as she got to the potato patch.

"Thelma, wait!" I called out.

She stopped running and turned to look at me.

"I hate this war! There is no food. There is no clothing or shoes. Everyone is scared to talk to each other, and if you are seen talking to a German, they think you are a traitor or a spy."

"You're right. It's not any fun. Mom knows it's hard on all of us, but it's even harder on her."

I took Thelma's hand, and we slowly walked toward the house. I tried to think of something to say that would comfort her. I wanted to tell her that I was helping by guarding the door and standing as a lookout for the local meetings, but I knew I couldn't.

"I can tell you that the Allies will attack Germany and drive them back to their homeland. The Germans will once again be defeated, and we will all get back to a more normal life."

Thelma stopped to turn and look at me.

"How do you know? Are you sure?"

I wanted to tell her about the Allies' landings that Mr. Dungvold had told me about, but I could not, at least not now.

"Have I ever lied to you before?"

Thelma thought for a second. "Yes, but just the once about Santa when I was little. So I will believe you this time, Trygve, but you'd better be right."

She hugged me and then continued toward the house. She was not as upset as she had been just a minute ago. After a few steps she turned around and said, "You'd better be right! If you have lied to me again, I will never forgive you."

I reassured her once more that I was right.

I heard Thoralf and Odd behind me and turned to see them coming down the hill with two baskets full of nuts.

Excitedly, Odd said, "Boy, you should have stayed. After you left they launched two more of those things."

"I am sure it won't be long before the Allies retaliate," Thoralf added.

Odd looked at him. "What do you mean?"

"Those buzz bombs looked to be heading for England," Thoralf explained. "They will not put up with that and will send bombers to take out the airport and the launcher. So far the fighting around here has been minimal, but I think we are about to get a little more attention."

"Tell Mom I am going to the nursery and then to Bestefar's grave," I told them. "I won't be long."

As I walked down the road near the prison camp, I noticed that some of the prisoners were right next to the fence. Their clothes hung from them, and their faces were thin and pale. With the food shortages, some of the guards allowed them to beg for food. Most of the prisoners were too proud to accept a handout, so they made little birds or other animals from things they found around the camp or while out working. They held them up in front of themselves or through the barbed wire, hoping to exchange their handiwork for an apple or anything to eat. I was told that the guards took a lot of the food the prisoners received but did allow them to eat some of it. I had shared some food once when the prison camp was first built but was quickly told by Mr. Ellenes that the Nazis watched who did this and then kept an eye on them after that, thinking that they might be trouble. I felt bad as I walked by with all those starving eyes looking at me, but I gave them nothing.

As I approached the nursery, I saw a truck with Gestapo markings parked in front of it. There were two guards by the truck, and two Gestapo officers were coming out the front door of the nursery, dragging Tore behind them. His hands were bound with rope, and the officers were hitting him on the back with batons for not moving fast enough. Mr. Olsen was right behind them, asking what Tore had done.

"Where are you taking him?" he demanded, holding his cane out in front of him. Seeing this, I turned and crossed the street to the graveyard, but not before I heard one of the officers respond.

"He is a spy, old man. He has been seen observing the airport and the docks. We know he is helping the resistance, and he will be shot after his trial."

The Nazis were getting more brutal with each passing day. Things were not going well for them in Europe, and now they resolved most issues by killing those they suspected of spying or fighting back. The two Nazis took Tore by the arms and threw him into the truck. With the truck pulling away, I didn't dare go to see Mr. Olsen. He, too, was probably being watched. Even though he was not so helpless, Mr. Olsen played the role well, and it kept the Nazis from suspecting him of anything.

I walked out of the graveyard and headed up the hill to see Mr. Ellenes. I was sure he would want to know about this. All I could think about was Tore and how the Nazis were probably going to shoot him.

When I arrived at Mr. Ellenes's store and walked up to the door, I was startled when it opened by itself. A large German soldier walked out eating an apple. I quickly moved aside to let him pass while saying, "Guten tag herr."

He was just a private in the regular army, and most of them left us alone, but I did not know if there were more soldiers inside and did not want to be seen as disrespectful. He replied, "Guten tag" and continued on his way.

I stood outside the door listening for anyone else who might be inside. Hearing nothing, I went in. The bell rang, and Mr. Ellenes turned to see that it was me. He stood behind the counter with an apple core in his hand.

"Trygve, you are not supposed to work today, but it's a good thing you stopped by. Tore stopped in on his way home yesterday looking for you and left you these tomatoes. He said you would know why. Is there something you need?" he asked.

"No, just stopping by on my way home."

I walked behind the counter and made the sign with my hand that I was taught to use whenever I had something important to say but was not sure who was around. The sign is made by placing the thumb on your left hand under your three middle fingers and on top of your pinky. He acknowledged the sign and put his hands up for me to wait and walked into the back room. A moment later he returned with Mr. Jakobsen and asked what it was I had to tell them. I looked at Mr. Jakobsen, unsure of what to do, and Mr. Ellenes said it was okay to tell both of them.

"The Gestapo took Tore from the nursery today! They had him tied up and were beating him as they dragged him to the truck! They said they were going to shoot him!"

I tried to say this as quietly and calmly as possible, but I got louder with each sentence. Mr. Ellenes had to put his hand over my mouth to stop me. Mr. Jakobsen looked at me thoughtfully before walking away and looking out the window. He didn't say a word. I was not sure what to make of this. He walked around the store for a minute, looking out all of the windows as if he were expecting someone. Then he walked back to me, put his hands on my shoulders, and with a very sincere look said, "I know I can trust you. Tore was one of my two."

At first, I was not sure what he meant, but it became very clear as he continued.

"I am part of the XU, the Unknown Underground. Locally we are organized into groups of two or three. Christian and I report to one person, and they and one or two others report to another person higher up. This way if someone is caught, they only know one or two names. This exposes only a few people should one be captured and succumb to the torture the Gestapo will put them through. I go one step further—I do not tell either of my two who the other is; that way each of them can name only me."

As he spoke, my wheels were turning. I always knew there was something going on when I worked as the gatekeeper, but this was different from those meetings.

"Why are you telling me this?" I asked.

Mr. Jakobsen replied, "Because Tore brought me reports of what was happening off the coast and at the airport. Now I need to replace him, and I'm asking you. You are fifteen now and have graduated from school, yes?"

I nodded my head. "Yes."

"You live at the top of the hill with a great view of the airport and the coast. Should you decide to help, I will hire you to work for me in town one day a week so no one will suspect you when you visit."

This was all so sudden. I nodded. "I can see the airport well, but the ships that I can see off the coast are too small for me to make out what they are."

Mr. Ellenes spoke up. "I can help you with that, but first I need to know if you want to be Tore's replacement. This is not something to take lightly. You know what they are doing to him, and they would not hesitate to do the same to you should they find out."

I looked at the tomatoes sitting on the counter and remembered planting the seeds with Tore and then moving the plants behind the greenhouse to hide them from the Germans. When did life become more about hiding things than sharing them?

"Yes," I said. I did not have to think long about this. "I want to help."

I had seen many things happen to people I knew because they were helping to fight back. It was now my turn to help, and I wanted to start right away.

Mr. Jakobsen stood by the front door while Mr. Ellenes walked me into the back where he proceeded to remove all of the firewood from the storage area beside the bread oven. He pulled out a few loose bricks from the back wall and reached into the void he had revealed. He fumbled around for a minute and pulled out a burlap bag. After looking in it, he folded it back up and reached into the void once more, this time pulling out a canvas bag. He opened it up and said, "This is it. This is what you will need. Here," he said, handing it to me, "hold this while I put everything back."

In the canvas bag was an old wood and brass spyglass. The rich mahogany was only lightly scratched, but the brass was heavily tarnished.

"Where did you get this?" I asked excitedly.

"It was given to me by my grandfather years ago. His brother, my great-onkel, was the Lista lighthouse keeper, and he left it to him when he passed away. It has been hidden in this wall since the Nazis arrived, along with some other items of value."

After Mr. Ellenes finished restacking the wood by the oven, he walked over and took the spyglass. Holding it in front of me, he said, "This is a triple-slide telescope, or spyglass in your case, as that is what you will be doing with it."

As we spoke, Mr. Jakobsen walked around the store, looking out each window to make sure no one would surprise us. Then he stepped out onto the front porch.

Mr. Ellenes continued. "Here, hold it and point it out the window. You focus it by sliding the outer eyepiece in and out. Try to focus it on the barn down the hill."

I slid the tube in just a little and, once in focus, it looked as if I could reach out and touch the barn. The telescope was lightweight, easy to hold, and about three feet long when fully extended. It was a beautiful piece of equipment and would make it easy to see and identify the ships offshore.

A few minutes later, Mr. Jakobsen came back inside. "Christian, does Trygve know how to use it, and have you told him what precautions to take?"

Mr. Ellenes shook his head. "He knows how to use it, but I have not told him anything else yet."

"Okay, let me take the telescope, and I'll walk home with Trygve to explain to him what he needs to know and answer any questions he may have."

Mr. Jakobsen slid the collapsed telescope into his pant leg and headed outside. I followed him out the door and said goodbye to Mr. Ellenes.

We started up the hill, and Mr. Jakobsen lit his pipe. Then, in a low voice, he began to tell me what he thought I needed to know.

"When we get near your house, I will give you the telescope. Hide it outside close to where you are going to use it. Use it only when you are alone and, of course, tell no one that you have it."

He puffed on his pipe and continued. "Pay close attention to where the sun is when you are using it because it will reflect off the lens and give away your position. The safest thing to do is to make sure the main lens is never in the sunlight. Keep it shielded, and use it when you are lying down with cover."

What was normally a short walk was made longer by our meanderingly slow pace. There was a lot of information to cover.

As we approached the Mikalsen's house we stopped. Mr. Jakobsen said that this was as far as he was going. He did not want my mom to see us together when he had no good reason to be walking me home, but if she did ask, I was to tell her it was because he had offered me a job. He looked at me gravely and reminded me to be careful.

"Tell no one, do not take any chances, and tell only me what you observe."

I thanked him for trusting me and told him that I would do whatever he needed me to do to get rid of the Nazis.

Mr. Jakobsen turned and started down the hill puffing his pipe, and I continued toward the house. When I arrived and saw no one around, I walked past the house up the hill to the overlook. Two of the larger rocks at the top of the hill had a small space between them, just large enough to hide the telescope, and it was right where I would be lying on the ground to view the airport and passing ships. I reached in, placing the telescope as far back as I could, and then placed smaller rocks in front of it to make it hard to see should someone even think to look in there. I was sure no one would ever find it.

September 20, 1944

On the first day of my job, Thoralf was working, and Odd and Thelma were in school. I told Mom I was going to the top of the hill to look out over the sea. She asked if I had finished all my chores and, as always, I had. I am not really sure why Mom let us all come up here. She even let Thelma come, and all she did was hide behind the rocks. One day I asked her about it, and she said that it was no more dangerous up here than it was in the front yard. I also think she let us because she was sentimental, remembering when she used to sit up here as a girl and dream of her future and better things. Whatever the reason, it made it easy for me to be alone and do my new part to help my country.

I was nervous as I approached the top of the hill. I had walked up here many times before, but knowing that I was here for a specific purpose made me both proud and jittery. I sat on one of the large rocks and slowly calmed myself down. After a few minutes of listening and looking around, I slid off the rock and crouched next to it. I looked around one more time and removed the smaller stones blocking the space between the two larger rocks. I slowly reached in and pulled out the canvas bag protecting the telescope. I looked around once more as I lay down with the left side of my body tight up against the warm rocks. My left ear was in line with the crag between them. This space collected all the sounds coming up from the house, making it easy to hear someone long before they reached where I was.

I was lying still for about an hour, being mindful of the sun and observing the airport and the occasional ship that passed by. The prisoners were working at the airport filling holes made from the last attack. The Germans were hard on them. They got very few breaks and most days worked from sunup to sundown. I could see they all were a lot thinner than when they had first arrived.

I turned to look back out at sea and noticed a squadron of planes. They were flying low just above the top of the waves. As they got closer, I saw through the telescope that they were British fighter-bombers, Mosquitos to be exact. It was thrilling to know what was going to happen before the Germans did. I watched through the telescope with great anticipation.

The aircrafts changed formation and were now spaced out in a straight line. I could see them opening their bomb bay doors. The high-pitched air raid siren began to scream out the warning. The prisoners all ran to dive into the nearby drainage ditch along the edge of the runway. Only a few German soldiers stayed to guard them, while most ran for protection near the gun emplacements or into the bunker that was built into the side of the hill. As the bombers approached their targets, they fired their wing guns briefly and then dropped their bomb. This was immediately followed by an abrupt turn. Each plane turned in a slightly different direction after dropping its bomb so that the German gunners on the ground would not be able to anticipate its course, making it less likely to be hit.

My heart was beating out of my chest when I noticed that one of the prisoners had slowly crawled over to the edge of the woods. I panned back with the telescope toward the drainage ditch to see that the German soldiers guarding the prisoners were all protecting themselves from the flying debris with their heads down. The prisoner at the edge of the woods suddenly got up and ran toward the dense trees, and I soon lost sight of him. With the bombing over, I quickly put the telescope back in its hiding spot and crawled around to the other side of the rocks before standing up. I knew Mom would be worried having heard the bombs, and if I did not return soon, she would be calling for me. I did not want to give her any reason to stop me from coming up here. As I walked down toward the house, I wondered what the escaped prisoner would do. Where would he go? How would he survive the cold winter once it arrived?

September 22, 1944

As Thoralf and I walked to work a couple of days later, we heard something in the woods just as we passed by the Swensen's house. When I turned to look, I saw a pair of legs disappear into the small hole left from the collapsed smokehouse at the back of their yard.

"Did you see that?" I asked. "There's a man climbing into the Swensen's smokehouse."

"See what?" Thoralf replied.

"That man! I am sure I just saw someone crawl into the collapsed smokehouse through that small hole."

"Are you sure it was a man and not an animal?" he said, shaking his head in disbelief. "I think you are just seeing things. You have been acting different lately. Do you have a girlfriend you are keeping from me?"

I stopped myself from saying no and instead quickly said, "Well, I do kind of like Mr. Olsen's granddaughter. She came into the nursery the other day, and Mr. Olsen introduced us. She is very nice and liked that I kept up Bestefar's grave."

"She's at least three years older than you." Thoralf said. "I knew it was something like that. You have been very quiet and not yourself the last few weeks."

I thought about what he said and knew that others might have also noticed a change in me. I needed to work on correcting this by making sure to have more everyday conversations with friends and family and more serious ones only with those whom I had sworn to help.

October 12, 1944

While in my spot at the top of the hill, I often saw the Germans' small coastal patrol boats known as VP-Boats. There were four that seemed to overlap the part of the coastline where I was stationed, and they slowly cruised up and down the shoreline looking for suspicious activity. On this day the sea was rough, and V-1605, The Mosel, looked to be having a hard time. The waves were breaking across its bow, and it appeared to be listing to port as it made its way east toward Farsund from just south of the Lista lighthouse Normally, when I saw the VP-Boats making this arc across my view, it took them no more than 10 minutes, but with today's conditions, this ship was taking much longer.

I shared what I saw with Mr. Jakobsen and, while I don't know specifically what he did with that information, I do know that a couple of days later, The Mosel was attacked by the Allies and sank just off the coast. I like to think that I played a small role in that.

October 25, 1944

It was a chilly, cloudy day, and the rocks I leaned against did not have a chance to warm up. As I watched, I did not see anything other than the normal German routines at the airport. I panned out over the sea one more time and was beginning to pack up when I noticed what looked like one of the local VP-Boats. It was a lot farther from shore than usual and seemed to be moving slowly. This piqued my interest, and I patiently waited.

When it got closer to the shoreline, it changed direction and turned to head up the coast toward Farsund. As it did, I could see that it was towing a submarine, and the telescope allowed me to clearly identify it as a U-985. Fortunately for them, the sea was calm. There were men manning its deck gun, two people visible atop the conning tower, and a few others on its deck. The sub must have had engine trouble nearby because a little boat like the VP would not normally travel too far from the coast by itself. I panned around the local area looking for anyone nearby and, seeing no one, packed things up and headed into town to see Mr. Jakobsen.

November 10, 1944

I once again found time to be by myself and set up the telescope to watch the airport and the surrounding sea, hoping to see something that would be helpful for our fight against the Germans. Most days there was very little to see other than the Germans' normal operations. It was cool out, and the wind coming up the hill was slightly damp. The rocks I lay against were warmed by the sun, making them quite comfortable despite the cool weather.

I had previously noticed the prisoners clearing a section of the woods near the airport. On this day, they were tying camouflage netting to the trees at the perimeter of the clearing, making it disappear to those who did not know where to look.

As time went on, I had developed a pattern to my observations. First, I looked at the area just down the hill for any stray Germans who might be patrolling. Then I slowly swept the airport and its surroundings and before scoping out the sea for any ships.

I did not own a watch, and when Mr. Jakobsen offered to give me one, I declined. It would have been too hard to explain to Mom, and if I left it with the telescope, it might not get wound often enough to keep good time. Fortunately, I remembered learning how to make a sundial in school. I had all but completely buried two medium-sized rocks for my noon reference points and had scratched the radii for each hour into one side of the canvas bag. I whittled several birch stakes, pointed on one end and flat on the other, to use as the gnomon that cast the shadow. I did not need to be very accurate, so this worked best for me. I could quickly set it up and take it down when needed and, since I always knew what time it was when I went to the hilltop, it was easy to set the shadow on the dial plate I had drawn on the canvas bag to the current time. I could record times within an accuracy of five minutes, and I knew that, from where I sat, due south was in line with the corner of the fence around the airport. I had good reference points for the bearing of ships at sea from 270 degrees due west to 135 degrees southeast.

That afternoon, I saw several trucks pull up to the camouflaged area. At first, I was not sure what they were carrying but knew it must be important to the Germans. A soldier signaled one of the trucks to turn around so that it could back up into the clearing under the camouflage. As it did, I could see inside the back of the truck, and it looked to be full of fuel drums.

Truck after truck pulled into the camouflaged area and then drove back out. I could see that they were empty when they pulled out because the Germans did not close the trucks' rear flaps. I made mental notes of how many trucks I saw to report to Mr. Jakobsen later. I never wrote anything down because, after the journal incident, I didn't want to be found with information on me. Mr. Jakobsen said that I had the best memory of anyone he knew, right down to the smallest detail. He said that I needed to relay only what type of uniforms were being worn and how many officers and enlisted men were there, but I told him that I would rather give him more than he needed to know than not enough.

May 6, 1945

This afternoon when I arrived home from work, I saw Odd sitting on the front stoop, and I saw Dr. Halversen's bike by the stairs. Thelma had been sick, but I didn't think it was worth a doctor's visit.

I asked Odd why the doctor was here, and he told me he was here to see Thelma and Mom.

"For Thelma and Mom? What happened to Mom?!" I exclaimed.

"Well, Thelma has these red bumps all over her and a fever of 102. Mom sent me to get the doctor, and while I was gone she hurt her leg. Apparently, she tripped and fell while getting water from the well to cool Thelma off. Bestemor heard her scream and found her lying on the ground. Bestemor was able to help her inside, and she put Mom in the guest room on the chair next to the bed where Thelma is resting. Bestemor told me all this when I returned with the doctor—she let him in and pushed me back out the door, so here I sit."

"Have you been able to hear anything through the door?" I asked.

"No. I think it must be bad because they have all been very quiet."

I reached to open the door and Odd said, "Bestemor told me to keep you and Thoralf outside when you came home, so I wouldn't go inside if I were you."

I released the knob, let out a sigh, turned around, and sat next to Odd. Mom had never been sick or hurt; neither had Bestemor. They always told us that living in the country combined with hard work kept us healthy. This had been true since Odd's fight with polio. That is, it had been true until now.

After what seemed like an eternity, the front door opened, and Dr. Halversen came out. "Your sister has scarlet fever," he told us. "Fortunately, it looks to be a mild case, and your mom and grandmother have been doing a good job keeping her fever down. Your mom, on the other hand, is not in good shape. I am fairly certain she has a fractured leg. Luckily she didn't break it. I made a splint out of some boards you had in the cellar and some bandages I brought. Boys, it's very important that she stay off that leg. Do not let her do anything. You need to help her with whatever she needs."

This was Mom he was talking about. We knew she was not going to listen, but we nodded and told him we would do our best. Dr. Halversen got on his bike, and before heading down the hill, he said, "I will try to come back in a few days to check on them if I can. As I am sure you are aware, with the war going so poorly for the Germans, there is a lot going on in town, so I will do my best, but no promises. Come get me if either of them gets worse."

May 8, 1945

I was at the top of the hill in the spot I had been watching and reporting from for months. There had been very little activity the past few weeks because the war seemed to be coming to an end.

In the distance, I heard the faint sound of an airplane and looked up to see a small plane approaching from the southwest. It was flying low and close to the water. As it approached the coast, it turned to head inland and then turned again to line up with the runway before finally landing. Once it was on the ground, I could see it was a Ju-52 German aircraft. The Ju-52 was used for passengers or light cargo, but this one didn't have any German insignias on it. In fact, it didn't have any marking on it at all. I quickly pulled out the telescope from its hiding place and assumed my position for observation.

When the plane came to a complete stop, it was met by a truck. I watched as three German officers emerged from the plane. Through the telescope, I could see there were two Luftwaffe generals and a Navy admiral. They took off their uniforms, put on German Navy ones for enlisted men, and then climbed into the truck. The airplane taxied to the end of the runway as the truck pulled away, heading toward the shore. I looked ahead to the lighthouse and could see two German Navy soldiers standing by a rowboat. As the truck approached them, one of the soldiers signaled out toward the sea, but I did not see any boats. When the truck made it to the rowboat, the three German officers got out of the back and into the boat. As the last of them was about to get in, he turned as if to shake hands with the truck driver, and I saw two quick flashes. I am fairly certain he killed the driver. He climbed into the rowboat, and they pushed off from shore. I was still not sure where they were going.

As all this unfolded, the Ju-52 took off and turned, heading back in the direction it came from. I still could not see any boat or small ship in the direction the rowboat was heading.

All of a sudden, there was a disturbance in the water, and then the conning tower of a submarine emerged from the sea. I could clearly see "U-977" on it. The rowboat was so close to the submarine when it surfaced that it rocked and was pushed away by the rushing water. Several sailors emerged from the sub, and one of them threw a line to the men in the rowboat. Once the line was caught, the rowboat was pulled tight to the sub, and all the men climbed up and into the vessel. The rowboat was left to drift away. With the sub slowly diving out of sight, the empty rowboat was momentarily caught in its draft but veered to the right as the last of the sub submerged and was soon out of sight. I quickly put everything away and jumped up to go and let Mr. Jakobsen know what I had seen.

In all the excitement, I did something I had never done before—I stood up without looking or listening to what was around me.

"AH! Where the heck did you come from?" shouted Odd as I rose from my observation spot.

"Where did you come from, and how long have you been up here watching me?" I demanded.

"I asked you first. Were you hiding up here just to scare me?" Odd asked.

"No, I was just sitting on the other side of the rocks and must have fallen asleep. How long have you been up here?" I asked again.

"I just got here. I thought I saw something big go under the water, maybe a submarine. Did you see anything?"

"Nope, I told you I was asleep. What did it look like?"

Odd scratched his head. "Now I am not sure what I saw."

"Maybe you saw a whale," I said.

"Yeah, a whale with pipes stinking out of its head." Odd rolled his eyes. "Are you nuts? Did you hit your head or something?" he scoffed. "A whale. Next you'll tell me that you saw Himmler or Goering or maybe even Hitler." Odd turned to head back down the hill. "A whale," he said again, shaking his head. "Now I have heard everything."

"Well, whatever you saw is gone now," I called after him. "I need to go into town. Tell Mom I will be back soon."

"Mom said to stay out of town," Odd replied.

"Then tell her I am going to see Mr. Ellenes."

Odd turned and looked at me as he continued down the hill. "Okay, but I know where you are really going."

"Just tell her," I said.

I walked past my house and, once out of sight, picked up the pace. At the fork in the road to go into town, I heard Mr. Ellenes calling for me. I turned to see him standing on the front porch of his shop, waving to me. I ran to see what he wanted, and he turned and walked back inside the store. I jumped onto the porch, skipping the stairs. The door was propped open, and as I ran inside, I bumped right into him on his way back out with two bags full of food.

"Trygve, take this," he said.

I could see past him inside, and there was nothing left. All the shelves were empty.

He pushed me back outside. "Here, take this," he repeated. "There are some loaves of bread and some cheese my wife made from goat's milk, along with a few other small items."

"What's this for? Where have all the goods from your store gone?" I asked.

Mr. Ellenes slowly pushed me across the porch and down the stairs. "Mr. Dungvold was just here and told me that the war is going to end soon and that the Germans, being the nasty people they are, will start burning everything and killing those who get in their way. Take this food for you and your family. Tell them that you need to go hide up in the mountains. The Germans will not go out of their way to chase any of us down. Go home now and get your family packed up and moving."

"But I saw something strange happen at the airport, and I need to go tell Mr. Jakobsen."

Mr. Ellenes grabbed me by the shoulders, looked me straight in the eye, and said, "You need to go home now. Nothing you saw is going to make any difference this late in the war. Go home and get your family some place safe away from town."

As I walked back to the house, I was not sure what we were going to do. Mom could not walk, and Thelma was still sick. As I thought through our options, I heard my name being called and turned to see Thoralf running up from behind me.

"What you got in the bags?"

"What are you doing coming home so early?" I asked.

"The Germans are closing down all the businesses in Farsund and told everyone to go home," he replied.

"Mr. Ellenes told me to take all this food and to get the family into the mountains because the Germans are going to burn everything."

"Then we need to hurry home. Give me one of those bags so we can run."

I handed one of the bags to Thoralf, and we ran up the hill to the house. As we got to the top step, the front door swung open, and Odd stepped outside with an empty water bucket. Thoralf and I ran past him and into the kitchen, placing the bags of food on the table.

"What, no hello? Just run right by me with bags of stuff and make me wonder what is in them," Odd said sarcastically.

Bestemor was standing by the stove and, seeing us, she turned and asked, "Where did you get all of that stuff?"

"Mr. Ellenes gave it to me. He told me to come right home and get everyone out of the house and into the woods to hide from the Germans. Mr. Dungvold told him that the war is about to end and that the Germans will start burning everything and killing those who are in their way."

Bestemor stood frozen in place for a few seconds. "How are we going to move your mother and Thelma?"

Thoralf replied, "You let Trygve and me figure that out. You and Odd pack up what you think we will need for a few days in the woods—just the essentials and what you and Odd can carry."

"We can take them to the hunting blind. There is enough room for Bestemor, Mom, and Thelma inside," I told Thoralf.

"That's what I was thinking. You get some of the fishing gear, matches, and the canteens. I will go outside and make Mom a crutch from a tree limb. The cane she is using now will not do well outside where we are heading."

As I started to run up the stairs, I heard Mom yell out, "What's all the commotion?"

"Ask Thoralf," I said quickly as I continued up the stairs.

"I will tell you when I come back inside," Thoralf yelled as he ran out the back door.

Mom had now hobbled to the doorway of the guest room and again called for Thoralf. Bestemor came from the kitchen and said, "Trygve said that we need to get into the mountains and hide from the Germans."

As I came back down the stairs and turned the corner, Mom stopped me in my tracks. "What did you tell your grandmother, and who told you?"

"Mr. Ellenes called me when I was walking by and gave me all this food. He said the Germans are going to start burning everything because they are about to lose the war."

Mom closed her eyes as she thought about what I had just told her. Thoralf ran back inside with the crutch he had made.

He handed me the crutch and instructed me to get everyone outside. He added, "I am going to tell the neighbors. I will meet you by the back door." he raced outside.

Bestemor and Odd were in the kitchen with everything packed up and ready to go. Mom headed into the kitchen with her crutch as I went to get Thelma. She was sleeping when I entered the guest room. As I gently shook her to wake her up, I noticed that her skin was wet and clammy, and she looked startled to see me.

"Hi, Trygve. What are you doing in here?" she mumbled.

"Come with me. We're all going into the woods to hide from the Germans."

"Okay."

I helped her climb out of bed, and she walked with me to the kitchen. She was not very sure-footed, having been in bed for the last four days and still not over her fever. I noticed Mom was sitting on the bench shaking her head.

"No, I will just slow you down. I will stay here. They will not shoot an injured old lady. Go without me. You all will have a better chance."

Thelma heard this and started to cry. "NO! We can't leave Mom, NO!" she was now shaking uncontrollably and becoming hysterical.

Thoralf came through the back door. "What is all this? Why are you all still inside?"

"Mom said she is not going because she will just slow us down," I replied.

"Mom!" Thoralf spoke sharply. "We are all going, or none of us are going. You decide."

This was the first time I had heard anyone other than Pop give her an ultimatum. She looked startled at first, but as Thoralf walked over and helped her up, she gave in. We headed out the back door, me helping Thelma, Odd helping Bestemor, and Mom with Thoralf at her side.

By now, night had fallen, and the sliver of moonlight was occasionally blocked by a passing cloud. Odd had the flashlight, but he was not to turn it on unless we told him to. This made our journey across the rough terrain of the open fields and woods long and slow. The houses we could see were all dark. I could hear people in the distance but could not see anyone. Most of what I heard was mumbling or breaking branches.

We had to stop to rest because, even with Thoralf's help, Mom was stumbling more than walking.

Mom shook her head and said, "I told you I should have been left behind."

"No, Mom, you were wrong," Thoralf told her.

"We all need to stay together," I added. "It is what's best for all of us. We are a family and need to stay that way."

After a few minutes, Thoralf asked, "Are we all ready to move? Trygve, help me get Mom up, and then go ahead of us to the road and make sure it is clear."

"Okay," I replied, even though it had been more of an order than a question.

I headed toward the road we would soon have to cross. Now that I was out in front, I realized the family was making a lot more noise traveling through the woods than if it had just been Thoralf and me. I knew I would have to tell them to be more cautious and quiet to make sure we were not seen or heard.

As I approached the road, I saw several trucks and motorcycles pass by, heading toward town. I had never seen so many vehicles this far out of town at one time. I slowly crept my way up to the edge of the road. Carefully sticking to the shadows, I stopped and listened and did not hear or see anything else coming down the road. I signaled to Thoralf, and he and the rest of the family made their way toward me. As soon as they caught up to me, we headed across the road, with Mom and Thoralf bringing up the rear.

Just as they made it across safely, I heard a horse whinny. I knew that sound; it sounded just like Freya. Everyone hid behind a tree, and I moved back toward the road. I could see two horses pulling a cart up the hill. It had to be—it just had to be Onkel Tarald. When the cart pulled up right next to me, I could see that it was. I stood up and walked into the road. This startled the horses and Onkel Tarald, but just for a second.

"There you are. I have been looking all over for you," Onkel Tarald said in that wonderful, reassuring voice of his. "Where is the rest of the family? The war is over, and the Germans have surrendered. I talked to Christian, and he told me what he instructed you to do. I knew you would head this way. You and Thoralf are two smart men." he smiled.

One by one, everyone stood up. Onkel Tarald jumped down from the wagon to help Mom. She and Bestemor sat in the front, and the rest of us climbed in the back. The war was over. It was hard to believe. On the ride home, Onkel Tarald said that we were all lucky to have survived.

"Many others were not, and they gave their lives so we could live," he said. "We need to remember those people and help their families. They have given more than anyone should have to give, and they did it just because it was the right thing to do."

We were all very quiet as we thought about what he had just said. I sat thinking about my neighbor, Mr. Swensen, and how his son took the blame for hiding the prisoner in their smokehouse, even though it was his father's doing. I wondered if I would ever see him again. Tore, whom I replaced as a coast watcher, did not survive. That could have been me. If I had been caught, what would the Nazis have done to my family? I was no longer feeling proud about what I had been doing, and suddenly I knew why more people did not resist the Germans. It was not because they were afraid of what would be done to them—it was because they were afraid of what would be done to their families. I knew then that I could not tell my family or anyone what I did to help. If Mom ever found out, she would never forgive me for putting the family at risk.

As we rode, the silence continued for several minutes. The horses' footfalls and the slight rattling from the undercarriage were interrupted by Odd.

"Thank you," he said into the darkness. "Thank you to all of those people."

The rest of us followed his lead, and Mom said a prayer of thanksgiving to all those who had given their lives.

May 9, 1945

The next morning, breakfast seemed to taste better. It was the same thing we had the day before—just bread and jam—but with the war over, it just tasted better. We thanked Bestemor and Mom for breakfast, kissed them on the cheek, and left for work. Thoralf was not sure if the furniture factory would even be there when he arrived, and I was not sure if there would be anything to clean or bake in Mr. Ellenes's store with everything emptied out, but we both wanted to see how things looked in and around town. It was a beautiful morning, mostly cloudy with the occasional drizzle and raindrops, but clear off to the west. As we walked by Mr. Swensen's house, he was outside hanging the Norwegian flag from the mast by his front door. The breeze was just enough to make it flutter.

"It's nice to see your flag again, Mr. Swensen. We will need to put ours back up when we get home," I told him.

"Yes, that is a good idea," Thoralf added.

"What do you think it will be like now that the war is over?" I asked my brother as we walked on.

"Well, I am sure it will be better, but I am not sure how long it will take. The war has changed a lot of things."

"Yeah, like you. Before the war, you would never have given Mom an ultimatum and definitely never would have told her she was wrong like you did last night."

"I know. I apologized to her this morning before you came down. She said it was okay and that I was right and that you and I were more men now than boys. She was glad about that, but said she did miss her boys."

"Mom said that? She thinks we are men?" I said. "Wow, who would have thought that?"

"Yes, she did. I am sure she will tell you when you get home today." Thoralf paused for a second and then added, "Well, maybe not."

"What do you mean?" I asked nervously.

"Well, you know, to be a man, you have to be able to ski through the woods without ending up in a snow bank," Thoralf replied, laughing as he jogged away from me.

I laughed. When he was a few feet in front of me, I called out. "Wait up. I have something for you."

I stood in front of him and then thanked him for telling me what Mom had said and for being a good brother and my best friend. I had never hugged my brother before, but this seemed like the right time, so I did. He smiled, patted me on the back, and turned to head toward work.

As I turned to start up the hill, I heard him say, "You still owe me for not telling Mom about your taking her shortcut when you tried to beat me to school."

I thought for a second, turned, and yelled back, "Nope, we are even. I never told Mom about the Gestapo officer wanting to shoot you for scuffing his boot."

"Okay, we are even for now," he conceded.

Turning around again to head to the store, I saw a large Norwegian flag hanging from the front porch. I also saw Freya tied to the rail along with another horse. When I entered the store, all the shop owners were there. They were laughing as they ate warm bread with butter, and the smell of tobacco was again heavy in the air. I was not used to seeing all these men in this store smiling and laughing.

"Sorry, I did not know there was a meeting today," I said as I turned to head back outside.

"No, no, you do not need to do that anymore. The war is over. Stay inside with us and have some bread," Mr. Jakobsen insisted.

"Why, thank you. I am still a little hungry."

"Don't thank me. It is every one of us in this room who should be thanking you, and me especially for what you did when we lost Tore. That was a huge commitment on your part," Mr. Jakobsen said while chewing.

"That's what I would like to talk to you about. Can you and I step outside?"

We headed onto the porch and closed the door behind us. The pipe smell followed us out, and all I could think about were my grandparents in Spangereid and if they were OK. I stood there with a blank look on my face.

"What is it you wanted to ask me?" Mr. Jakobsen asked, lighting his pipe.

I shook my head to clear my thoughts, looked around, and began.

"You see, I was glad to help and was probably a little naïve at the time about the danger I put my family in. You cannot tell anyone that I helped you. If word got back to my mother, she would be very upset with me."

"I understand, but like many other coast watchers, you did a great service to your country and should be proud of your contributions," he replied.

"I am proud, but you understand, now is probably not the best time to tell her about it. I am sure there will come a time to tell her, but just not now."

"If that is what you want, then I will not mention your name. I will tell Christian and Mr. Jaartag not to either."

"Mr. Jaartag, the man who owns the furniture factory?" I asked.

"Yes, that's him. Why do you ask? Do you know him?" Mr. Jakobsen looked puzzled.

"That's where my brother has been working for the last two years. Do you think he told my brother what I was doing?"

"I am sure he didn't," Mr. Jakobsen said with confidence.

"Why did he know about me? You said that only you and Mr. Ellenes would know."

"Yes, but I guess I can tell you now that I gave the information that I received from you, Tore, and the other coast watcher to Mr. Jaartag. In fact, after Tore was captured and I needed a replacement, I mentioned your name. Mr. Jaartag said if you were anything like your brother, you would be a good choice. I was not sure how he knew that, but now I do. You may want to talk to your brother. Ask if he helped or knew how the information left the furniture factory."

"I don't think I want to ask him," I said slowly. "He will tell me if he thinks I need to know. Thank you for keeping my secret, Mr. Jakobsen. Thank you."

As we turned to go back inside, all of the other shop owners were leaving. Each of them shook my hand and thanked me for being the gatekeeper during their meetings. I thanked them and said I was glad to help, even if I had gotten a reputation as the slowest repairman in town.

When everyone left, I went inside to a once-again empty store, and I could hear Mr. Ellenes talking to Onkel Tarald in the back room. I went back there to find the two of them taking several loaves of bread out of the oven. Several more were already out cooling.

"Where did you get the supplies to bake all this bread?" I asked.

"Well, yesterday when you came by, your Onkel had just left. I had asked him if he would take what supplies I had up to his place and hide them. He said yes but asked if I could keep a few things back for his sister. That is what I gave you," he replied.

"Who are you making all this bread for?" I asked.

He shuffled the remaining loaves around in the oven. "They have unlocked the prison camp, but the prisoners have nowhere to go, and they have nothing. My wife made as much butter as she could, and your Onkel brought some jars of jelly. We are going to take all this bread down to them. It is not much, but they need to have something to eat."

I asked if they needed help, and Mr. Ellenes said they were almost done for the day. He added, however, that I should show up early tomorrow to put what little he had back up on the shelves and to help bake more bread for the prisoners.

June 4, 1945

With the war over, it was time to reunite the family. Thoralf and I were going to Oslo to visit the U.S. Consulate. When we needed German identification papers at the start of the war, Bestemor had replaced our baptismal certificates with falsified Norwegian ones. Now that it was time to go to the consulate, Mom retrieved the original certificates from her hiding place underneath a loose floorboard under the stove and gave them to us. She still had the burn scar on her arm from bumping the underside of the stove in her hurry to retrieve them some five years ago. We took them from her, kissed her and Bestemor goodbye, and headed to Farsund to catch the ship to Oslo.

As we walked up the gangplank, everyone was very friendly. With the war over, it was taking some time for things to get back to normal, but that didn't dampen the festive mood. After what we all had been through, a few minor inconveniences—like having to stand the entire trip to Oslo—were nothing. It was great to be on the sea again.

Thoralf and I leaned against the railing facing aft and looked back toward the shore as the ship left the harbor.

"I can't wait to get to America to see Pop. Do you think he has changed much?" I asked Thoralf.

"No, I'm sure he looks the same. It's all of us who have changed. It has been almost ten years since we have seen him," Thoralf replied.

"Yes, it has and he's never seen Thelma. Well, he's seen pictures, but those were from when she was little. He's going to be very surprised when we get to America." I paused for only a minute and then asked, "Do you think the war changed us?"

Thoralf looked at me with confusion. "What do you mean? It changed everyone. We all did what was needed to survive. I am sure you did things you wouldn't have done during peace time."

What did he mean by "we all did"? I knew I could trust Thoralf, but I could not bring myself to tell him what I had done during the last years of the occupation. Not then. It wasn't the right time, and if I asked him what he did, he was going to ask me, too. I wondered whether there would ever be a right time to tell anyone.

"Well," he continued, "I saw a lot of Mr. Jakobsen at the furniture factory. Did he ever tell you why he was there so often?" he looked at me.

I thought quickly and said, "He did tell me he was having a desk made once, but I'm not sure if it was ever finished. He was very picky about things."

I hoped my answer was believable, but I knew Thoralf knew something that he was not telling me. I excused myself to find the head of the ship and did not see Thoralf again until we came to the dock.

When we arrived in Oslo, it was crowded. There were a lot of people waving and looking for family. Most people were coming to visit relatives that they had not seen since the start of the war. One gentleman I talked to had been traveling from Oslo to Bergen to see his brother when the war began. He had stopped in Stavanger to visit a friend on the way when the Germans attacked, and he was forced to stay with this friend until the end of the war.

He did tell me that he was able to secretly send a letter to his wife and children and received one back after almost two years. Two years, he repeated, but he was all smiles now and could not wait to get off the ship. His family thought he had been killed in the attack, as Bergen, Stavanger, and Oslo were among the major cities first targeted by the Germans.

Thoralf and I waved back to the people on shore as we slowly made our way off the ship. We did not know whom we were waving to, but everyone was so happy that we just wanted to be part of it. When we reached the bottom of the gangplank, we headed straight to the consulate. Thoralf did not want to waste any time. The streets were crowded near the port, but they thinned out as we walked along the stone streets away from the harbor. It was about two miles from the port to the consulate, but it was an enjoyable walk. We stopped at a fruit cart for some apples. Wearing the new gray suits Mom had made for us, topped off with our ivy-styled flat caps, I felt important when one of the cart vendors asked where we were going and I got to reply, "To the U.S. Consulate."

"What business do you two have there?" the man asked.

Thoralf was flirting with a girl at the bread cart next to us as I replied, "My brother and I were born in America and moved here when we were very young, but the Germans came before we could all move back."

"Well, I hope you are able to go back soon," he replied.

I thanked him, turned, and tapped my brother on the shoulder. "Thoralf, we need to get going."

Thoralf was paying for a loaf of bread and some cheese.

"Thanks, Inger," he said with a silly grin as I pulled him away. "Maybe I'll see you again when I head back home."

"Thoralf, why did you buy that? I got the apples for us to snack on. Mom said not to waste our money and to buy only what we need," I reminded him.

"I'm not sure why I bought it. I was talking to her one minute, and the next thing I knew, she was handing me bread and cheese and telling me that would be 25 cents, so I paid her."

He said this with a dazed look and big smile. I shook my head. Neither of us had time for a girlfriend during the war, but Thoralf was easily swayed by a pretty smile.

"You know, if the German soldiers had been girls, I don't think you would have survived the war."

The walk seemed quick, and everyone we talked to was very pleasant. There was only one small detour when we got lost momentarily, but we quickly got back on track after stopping someone to ask for directions.

Neither of us had ever been to Oslo, or any other big city for that matter, so there was a lot to see. The buildings did not have a lot of damage—mostly bullet holes and a few big chunks of debris every now and then. Based on Mr. Dungvold's stories, I had expected more.

When we arrived at the consulate, there was a line out the door and down the stairs onto the sidewalk.

Thoralf asked the man at the end of the line, "Excuse me, sir, is this the line to get into the American Consulate?"

"Yes, it is, sir," he replied.

I smirked and said, "He called you 'sir.'"

Thoralf looked at me and scowled, and then he asked the man in line, "How long have you been waiting here?""

"About an hour. When I got here the line was down the street to that corner, but that was before they opened the doors." The man pointed to the corner about 50 feet away.

"Thank you, sir."

Thoralf turned and said to me. "An hour. He has been here an hour and only moved 50 feet. How far do you think we are from the door?"

"Maybe 100 feet," I guessed.

"So that's two hours just to get to the door and maybe another hour inside. I guess it's a good thing I bought this bread and cheese for us to snack on," Thoralf said with a big grin.

"Yes, it's a good thing that pretty girl knew there was going to be a line here. Is that what you were asking her about? If she knew if there was going to be a line at the consulate?"

"Oh, be quiet. Just be happy we are prepared for this wait and we won't have to get out of the line because we are hungry."

When we finally made it to the front door some two hours later, there was a man sitting at a desk taking people's names and asking what business they had there. He then gave them a number and instructed them to sit in the waiting area in the next room. After receiving our number, Thoralf and I walked toward the waiting room. We stopped in the doorway, took a quick look around, and saw only two empty seats next to each other. I looked at him, and he at me, and we both ran toward them. As in our youth, we were both headed to the same one. This time I won. Everyone in the waiting room chuckled because Thoralf ended up sitting on my lap. He laughed and then slid off my lap into the empty seat next to me, saying, "I should have fed you more of the bread. That would have slowed you down."

We sat patiently for another hour or so until our number was called. When we heard it, we stood up and were directed to an office down the hall and told to knock and walk in. We had agreed that Thoralf was going to do all the talking. I was only there to answer any specific questions they might have for me. Thoralf knocked on the partially opened door, and we walked in and sat down. This time we did not fight over who sat where. Thoralf picked his seat, and I took the other.

"Hello, gentleman. I am Mr. Johnson. What can I help the two of you with today?"

"Well, Mr. Johnson," Thoralf began. "We are American citizens, and we were stuck here during the war. We want to get travel papers to go to America to live with our father. He is there waiting for us."

"What about your mother?"

"We would love to take our mother, brother, and sister with us," Thoralf responded.

"Were they born in America also?"

"No, our brother and sister were born here in Norway, and Mom was born here also. Mom lived in America from 1925 'til 1931, but she had not finished becoming a citizen."

Mr. Johnson sighed. "Well, I would love to tell you that they can go with you, but they cannot. The immigration laws changed in 1934, and your mother will have to reapply. It will be at least two years before she, your brother, and your sister will get a visa, but the two of you can go as soon as you can get passage."

He looked down at the paperwork in front of him, thought for a second, and added, "Thoralf, I see you will be 18 soon. You will need to get back before you turn 18, or you, too, will be subject to the new immigration laws."

He handed Thoralf some paperwork and told him to fill it out.

Thoralf looked at it and asked, "What is this for?"

"As an American citizen, you need to register for the draft," Mr. Johnson replied.

"But the war is over," Thoralf said in a surprised voice.

"Yes, but they are letting combat troops go home and replacing them with new draftees. If drafted, you will probably be sent to Germany for the occupation of their country until things are sorted out there. Do you speak any German? They especially need soldiers who speak German."

My brother sat there frozen, and I was not sure what to do. There was a minute of silence, and then he signed the papers. A few moments later, we had the paperwork we needed to see our father. We thanked Mr. Johnson and headed outside.

"You know it would be just my luck to get drafted as soon as I get to America," Thoralf said, shaking his head.

"Mom will probably want us all to stay together anyway. She is not going to break up the family now. Two more years is not that long," I replied.

"No, I am sure Mom will tell us to go and to go soon. I am fairly certain she knew this was going to happen and hinted at it to me before we left," Thoralf said, his voice reflective.

June 1, 1945 - May 14, 1949

Thoralf was right—when we returned home from Oslo, Mom told us that we needed to go to America right away. While we were gone, she had written Pop to let him know to expect us in a few weeks and to make sure that he had room for us. We received a letter from him two weeks later with his new address in Washington, D.C., along with the phone number for the boarding house he and Mr. Haug were staying in. They had moved to D.C. because Mr. Haug wanted to start his own business, and there was too much competition in New York City. Mr. Tollison, their other housemate and companion, did not move with them—he had proposed to and later married Mrs. Tharaldsen, the widow of their late friend who owned the boarding house.

In preparation for our departure, Thoralf and I helped stock as many things in the root cellar as we could. We cut peat with Onkel Tarald one more time and by now had become so quick at it that, with Odd and Thelma's help, Onkel Tarald no longer did most of the heavy lifting and had time to tell us stories as we worked. This was one of the many things I knew I would miss when I left.

Two days later, Onkel Tarald came with Ord and Freya pulling the hay cart to take Thoralf and me to Farsund, where we would catch the first boat to Kristiansand; from there we would catch a second boat to New York City.

It was an eight-day trip on a crowded ship with little space to yourself. When we finally made it to New York, Pop was waiting for us at the customs and immigration exit. He was holding a handwritten sign above his head that said, "My Sons." He could have just put our names on the sign, but what he had written made me feel as though I was more than just a name to a father I had not seen in more than 10 years.

After long handshakes and a quick hug, we walked to the bus station. Our conversation was nonstop, full of questions and answers that continued for most of the bus ride to Washington, D.C., until Thoralf and I fell asleep. When the bus arrived at the station, Pop woke us up. We headed outside, got on a streetcar, and rode to the boarding house, where we met Mrs. Wilson, the proprietor. Pop's room in the house was small and now, with three of us in it, even smaller, but the food Mrs. Wilson made was amazing. Her husband had died in the attack on Pearl Harbor. Along with running the boarding house, she had a job as a cook at the Statler Hilton just a few blocks from the White House. Pop knew we needed to buy a house before Mom, Odd, and Thelma arrived.

Now that we were in Washington, D.C., Thoralf and I immediately went to work for Mr. Haug's newly formed Southeastern Flooring Company. We joined the Carpenters Union and started our apprenticeship. With the two of us added to the payroll, Mr. Haug now had seven employees.

It would be two years before our family would all be together. During that time, Thoralf and I saved as much money as we could and gave it to Pop as a present when we found the house he wanted to buy. It had only two bedrooms, but it had a big backyard for a garden. Thoralf and I finished off the attic and moved up there. We even had enough space for Odd when he arrived. Thoralf said we should have put his bed in the basement next to the furnace just to see his expression, but Pop wouldn't let us. I bought some tulip bulbs and other flowers and planted them along the fence. Thoralf bought a cherry tree and planted it in the backyard so Mom could see it from the kitchen window.

When Mom, Odd, and Thelma finally arrived, the three of us went to New York to meet them. My high expectations were outdone the moment I first saw them. Mom was as pretty as I remembered, but Odd was now a man, and Thelma was even prettier than before. It was at that moment that I realized how Pop must have felt when he first saw Thoralf and me.

On the ride home, I could not imagine anything being more emotional than our reunion, but that was outshined, too, this time by the moment we pulled up to the house. The look on Mom's face was pure joy. She sat in the car for a moment, frozen, and then she started to cry. She kept saying, "It's beautiful, it's beautiful, it's all so beautiful." At first I thought she was talking about the house, but soon I realized that it was at that moment—with the war over, her family safe and all together, and a place to call her own—that she could finally let her guard down.

August 1, 1999

For the first time in more than three hours, silence fell. I almost could not believe what I had just heard. My father had just told me what he had done during the war, and if I had heard it from anyone else, I would not have believed it. I asked him why he had never told anyone and he said, "Most people do things because it is the right thing to do at the time. In my case, I was angry with what the Germans had done to my friend Tore and made a decision to help, without thinking about what it might mean for the rest of the family if I were caught. Once I said yes, though, I did not want to go back on my word, and I did the best job I could. I believe my regret is why I was always so cautious and probably the main reason I was never found out."

I replied, "Well, I think you made the right decision, and I am sure your parents would have thought so, too."

The two of us stood up to head back down the hill, but first my dad bent over and looked between the two rocks. He stood back up and said, "Nope."

I asked him what he was looking for and he replied, "Well, a few days after the end of the war I managed to come up here alone to retrieve the telescope, and it was gone. I never did figure out what happened to it and did not want to ask anyone about it. When I told Mr. Ellenes I would pay him for it, he told me that I had already paid for it by doing what I had done."

As we walked down the hill—there was no jogging this time—my father looked relieved now that he had told someone what he had done during the war. He opened my eyes to a side of my family that will stay with me forever. The rest of my time in Norway was uneventful in comparison.

The story continues at Kurtblorstad.com, where you can find the following:

- My family's recipes for food items mentioned in this book,
- Photographs of the places described in the book.
- Photographs of the people who are the real-life models for the characters in the book.